# ANOTHER WAR

# ANOTHER WAR

# Simon Morden

First published in England in 2005 by
Telos Publishing Ltd, 5A Church Road, Shortlands,
Bromley, Kent BR2 0HP, UK

www.telos.co.uk

Telos Publishing Ltd values feedback. Please e-mail us
with any comments you may have about this book to:
feedback@telos.co.uk

This Edition 2016

Cover by Simon Moore

ISBN: 978-1-84583-947-5

*Another War* © 2005, 2016 Simon Morden.

The moral rights of the author have been asserted.

British Library Cataloguing in Publication Data.
A catalogue record for this book is available from the
British Library.

Dedication

For my own little horrors,
without whom I'd get so much more done,
but nothing would be worth doing.

# 1

Thacker would normally have flirted with the nurse. She was neat in her blue uniform, a white belt accentuating her hourglass figure. Perhaps she would have expected it of him, also in uniform, pips on his shoulder, a lean strength about him that told of experience and confidence.

Today wasn't the moment. He felt uncomfortable and hurried. He wasn't the sort of man to turn up at an old people's home in an army Land Rover, complete with a squad of men with rifles. Neither was he the type to rest his hand on the butt of his pistol as he invaded the too-warm foyer and asked politely to see Miss Emily Foster.

Give her her due, the nurse the nervous receptionist called acted calmly and coolly. She didn't allow guns inside her establishment. He apologised, but said those were his orders. She told him that telephones had been in common usage for several years. He apologised again.

Then he said it was an urgent matter of national security, and she relented.

The nurse led him down a corridor rich with paintings and flowers to a conservatory full of bright summer morning light. The view swept down a long hillside, over the town, and across the sea. On a clear day, France was visible as a thin dark streak on the horizon.

There were thickly upholstered armchairs and hothouse plants. It was as warm as the Algarve, but the slight figure in one of the chairs wore a thick cardigan and trembled as if cold.

'You'll have to leave,' he said to the nurse.

'No,' she said simply.

'This conversation will be covered by the Official Secrets Act. You haven't signed it, and you will have to leave.'

'Then find me a copy to sign. I'm staying, and that's that.'

He looked at his watch. Time was running out, of that he was certain. The unknown factor was how much time he had in the first instance. 'Stand by the door. Make sure no one comes in, and please, face the other way. I need to show Miss Foster some things that you cannot see.'

He was so serious, so urgent, that he managed to shock the nurse into compliance. She nodded, and took her position.

Carefully and slowly, he sat down next to Emily Foster. She made no sign that she was aware of him. She stared out to sea with milky blue eyes, and the sun full in her face managed to illuminate the bones under her parchment-thin skin.

He unbuttoned his battle smock. He was sweating from the heat and from nerves. Nothing in his extensive training had prepared him for this whole insane situation.

'Emily? Emily Foster?'

She turned, slowly, her head trembling all the while.

'My name is Major Thacker. I'm with the army. Do you understand?'

Emily Foster thought, and then she remembered.

'Army?' she said. Her voice was very quiet, almost shy. 'Like Robert was? He was a captain, you know.'

She leaned slightly forward, holding her hand clawed with arthritis towards him.

Thacker took it in both his huge hands and gently

pressed it. 'Just like Robert,' he said. 'It's Robert I'd like to talk about, Miss Foster.'

'Oh dear. It's a very long time since I saw Robert.'

'I know.' Thacker felt that as long as he held her hand, he would hold her attention. 'Do you remember Henbury Hall at all?'

'I'm a hundred and five, you know.'

'Yes, I do know, Miss Foster. I know a lot about you. And about Robert, and Doctor Nathaniel Middleton. But I don't know enough to help me. Will you help me, Miss Foster?'

'A long time since I saw Robert.'

It had been a mistake to come here, thought Thacker. He was getting nowhere and he didn't have the time to waste. One last try.

He let go of her hand and reached inside his battle smock and took out an aerial photograph. 'This is Henbury Hall, Miss Foster. Do you know it?'

He gave her the glossy print and she brought it to within two inches of her nose. The tremble in her hands made reflected light dance across her face.

'You must be mistaken, dear. You see, Henbury Hall vanished.'

'On the second of August, 1919, at roughly ten thirty in the morning. But at quarter to seven yesterday evening, it came back. We don't know where it's been for the last eighty years, but we'd like to find out.'

'It came back?' she said, and started to cry. 'Oh Robert.'

Thacker slid his finger between the old woman's face and the photograph. 'This is the main hall, yes? What's this collection of buildings here?'

'I miss my Robert. I missed him all my life. I was cruel to him.'

'Miss Foster? Before I can send my men in to see

what happened to Robert, I need your help.' He found a cloth handkerchief and delicately dabbed her tears away.

'The stables,' she said. 'Those were the stables.'

He seized his chance. 'And this?'

'Some sort of workshop. Garden tools and the like. Robert lost his leg in the war, you know. The Great War.' She sighed.

'Where was Robert's room?'

'Oh, on the ground floor. He didn't hold with stairs, afterwards. We were all in the east wing. Kitchen, drawing room, dining room. The servants lived up on the third floor. Little rooms. Poor Adele. She was a maid.'

Thacker knew. 'Yes, Miss Foster.'

'So few people in such a big house. Robert's brother was killed in the war. Such a pity. So many gone.'

'Were there cellars, attics?'

'Yes, and yes. Not very big. I looked once. That was all. Tell me, what ever happened to Doctor Middleton?'

'He died about fifty years ago, Miss Foster.'

'Ah, I'm the last. That's because I'm so very old.'

'Yes, Miss Foster. Is there anything else you think I might need to know?'

She looked again at the photograph. 'I loved it there. It was beautiful in a sad sort of way. Such a long time ago.'

Thacker thought the moment had passed. He took the print away from her feeble grasp and put it back in his battle smock. 'I'm sorry to bring back difficult memories, Miss Foster. I'll leave you now.'

'Yes, yes. Poor Robert. If you find him, tell him I still love him.'

'I'll tell him, Miss Foster. Goodbye.' He got out of the chair and strode over to where the nurse was standing, half turned away. It was something, he supposed.

'Is it about that awful plane crash last night?' she said.

Thacker remained stone-faced. 'Nothing that you've heard must leave this room. If it does, I'll know, and so will my superiors.'

She looked at him squarely, faintly amused. 'Is that supposed to be a threat?'

He shrugged. 'I assume so. More of a statement of fact. I think you'd disappear more thoroughly than Henbury Hall was supposed to have done. That'd be a shame. You're very pretty.' He hated this part of his job: all so bloody cloak-and-dagger.

Her smile slipped as he walked on, back down the corridor, into the foyer with its armed men. He summoned them to his side with a wave of his hand, and they flanked him as he closed the distance to the Land Rover.

'Tell the helicopter to stand by. I'm going back to Oxfordshire immediately.'

'Sir.'

He got in beside the driver, who waited for the last door to slam shut before spinning his wheels on the gravel drive. When they were on their way, he took out the photograph again, and pointed to each part in turn, memorising the location and the function of each building, before turning to the main house and mentally labelling it.

Quite why he had been chosen over everyone else escaped him.


He was to brief twenty men inside a marquee that had been erected a mile inside the exclusion zone. He had a trestle table, a whiteboard, and an overhead projector. Somewhere outside was a generator thrumming away, and engineers were still stringing together lights from the plastic crate by the tent flap.

He waited for them to finish, leave, and for the guard to check that there was only Thacker inside. As the men filed in, each carrying a folding chair, Thacker busied himself laying out his notes on the table, mostly brittle, yellowing pages from the box file that was stamped Top Secret in fading red. Each sheet he took out was also stamped, together with strict instructions: No Copies To Be Made. There were other things, too, things in stoppered bottles, sealed with wax and notarised with peeling labels written in a fine, spidery hand.

He set them out at the far end of the table, together with the hasty report on them from Porton Down.

The last man in was the only one present out of uniform: the Ministry man Thacker knew only as Dickson, someone from MI5 who outranked him but never behaved like he did.

Thacker watched him close the tent flap and cross his arms. He nodded, and Thacker began.

'There'll be time for questions afterwards. I want you to all listen very carefully, because this isn't a scenario we've trained for before. Some of the facts may surprise you: they did me. Doesn't mean they're not true.'

He looked at their faces, young, eager, a little puzzled. He prised the lid off the black marker pen, and wrote at the top of the whiteboard, 'Henbury Hall'. Below the title he put three dates: 1834, 1919, and Yesterday.

'In 1834, Matthew Henbury, a railway magnate, purchased six hundred and fifty acres from the Bishop of Oxford. Henbury Hall was completed five years later, and the man made a peer of the realm five years after that. In 1919, Henbury's grandson, Robert, had returned to the hall following the death of his elder brother Edward, in the First World War. Robert himself was wounded at Ypres, losing a leg.

'On the night of the thirtieth of July, 1919, Robert Henbury's horse was killed in the stables. No other animal was harmed. A contemporaneous report by a Dr. Nathaniel Middleton, FRS, concludes that …' Thacker's hand hovered over the papers in front of him, alighting on Middleton's treatise. '"That the whole body of the creature had every calorie of heat removed from it in an instant, to the effect of freezing every part of it inside and out. Death must have been instantaneous, for the beast stood as if still sleeping in its stall, and entirely without signs of injury or distress."'

'Things get a little murky from now on. We only have Middleton's second-hand account from a statement he gave to the police. On the night of the first of August, a woman employed by Henbury as a maid appears to have died in the same way. She was found on the morning of the second by the butler. She was in bed, frozen solid. Middleton was summoned to the hall and told to drive the rest of the household to safety. Somewhere in this, the butler has died too, but how, we can't say. Middleton drove the three servants and Robert Henbury's nurse to the nearby village of Isherham. He left behind Robert Henbury, Jack Henbury – Robert's cousin – and a man called George Adams, who acted as Henbury's valet.

'A police car was sent from Oxford, but on arrival, found … nothing. Nothing as in, no hall, no estate, nothing, not even the ground on which the buildings had been. As if I took a map, cut a hole five miles across in it, then drew the edges together to make the hole itself disappear.'

Thacker turned on the overhead projector, and angled the square of light onto the whiteboard. A little leaked over the edges onto the canvas of the marquee, but not enough that people outside could see any coherent images.

'This is an Ordnance Survey map from 1910. Note the position of Henbury Hall, and specifically this road and this river.' He gave them a few seconds to soak in the detail, then swapped the image for a more contemporary map. 'This is the same area from a map made in 1982. Note the absence of Henbury Hall, the abrupt termination of the road here and here, and the lake here with an outlet at right angles to the original stream. I could show you pictures of walls that start suddenly, strange cliffs that appear halfway across a field, a tree where one half of it is missing. Henbury Hall vanished, and objects that were five miles apart one day, were touching the next.'

Thacker turned the projector off, and tapped the third date with his pen.

'Yesterday, for some reason, Henbury Hall came back. We need to find out why, and how, and who. There are aggravating factors: at the precise moment Henbury Hall appeared, United Airlines flight nine-thirty-seven London Heathrow to Chicago was overhead with one hundred and thirty-seven passengers and crew. Their remains are spread out in a mile-long geometrically precise arc on the east side of the site, and the Americans want access to the wreckage now. For obvious reasons, we can't let them.

'This situation will not go away if we ignore it. On the pretext of the plane carrying hazardous waste, we have cordoned off a very large area. Sooner or later, that cordon will be breached. We have to ascertain before then whether or not anything inside the Henbury Hall estate poses a risk.

'We're all trained in handling and deactivating chemical and biological weapons. We know how to take precautions. We are also soldiers. We know how to work together as a team, watch each other's backs, and neutralise any threat we may come across.'

He looked at their faces again: still young, but not so eager now. Puzzlement had turned to fear. Eyes were wide and white, mouths open and dry. Some fidgeted, clasping and unclasping their fingers, pulling on their chins and ears and noses, glancing left and right to see if anyone else believed this nonsense. Others were stock still, minds numb, hearing but not understanding, seeing but not remembering.

'Time is critical. Aside from the American dimension, Henbury Hall has been exposed to the air for some thirty-six hours. Any wind-borne chemical or pathological agent will have already been released. Winds have been light, and fortunately, no rain as yet. But birds have wings, and so does bad news.'

He turned the projector back on, and put a fresh acetate on it: taken from the aerial photo of the hall. 'We have had one break. Robert Henbury's nurse is still alive, and still compos. We have a sketchy idea of what the inside of the building used to look like – though that might have changed in the intervening years. I want you to look very carefully at this picture.' Thacker made a dismal attempt at humour: 'I'll be testing you on it later.' He walked away from the screen, and Dickson joined him by one of the slowly undulating walls.

'Was Emily Foster any use?'

Thacker rubbed his palms together slowly, grinding the sweat down. 'Better than nothing. Worse than I hoped. Her mind wandered rather – I suppose her short-term memory isn't what it used to be – but she was quite lucid when I talked about Robert Henbury. She said she still loved him.'

Dickson tapped out a cigarette and offered the packet to Thacker.

'I'm a biological weapons expert, Dickson. I'm hardly likely to take half a dozen plant-based carcinogens orally.' Thacker pressed his hands even harder together, so that he didn't reach out involuntarily and take one.

'Suit yourself,' said the Ministry man, and lit up. He took a long drag, held it, and breathed out through his nose. 'The Foster woman. Anything else?'

Thacker thought for a moment. 'Yes. Yes there was. She said she had been cruel to him. Struck me as odd at the time. According to Middleton, she and Henbury were engaged.'

'Perhaps she felt she should have stayed.'

'Not that. Some sustained cruelty. Earlier. I have no idea if it's at all important. Like everything in this bloody awful mess.'

'You should plan for everything.'

'I don't have the time, men or resources to do that. I can only plan for what is likely, and currently, I haven't a clue what to expect from a rematerialised neo-gothic Victorian country estate.' Thacker gave a tight-lipped smile. 'Any suggestions gratefully received.'

Dickson puffed away furiously. 'You'll think of something.'

'We'll end up with standard army procedure: straight down the middle, lots of smoke.'

'Anything from Porton Down?'

'Anything new? The grass and tree samples are clear. No known or unknown pathogens or chemical agents. They're just very, very dead, like they've been locked in a dry, dark room for eighty years. Brittle. Just turns to dust. If the wind gets up it'll be all over the south of England in a matter of hours. A good shower of rain will wash it away. It's only still on the ground through force of habit.'

'I have to get back to London tonight. What should I be telling the minister?'

Thacker took off his cap and rubbed at his scalp. 'You could make something up about how it's all under control.'

'That's the politicians' job. I'm a civil servant. They'll get the truth from me.'

'Good for you, Dickson. Tell him we're going in at first light with every piece of scientific equipment we can carry and some heavy ordnance just in case.' Thacker leaned closer. 'Tell him it's important that some sort of failsafe is arranged. And a failsafe for that, too.'

Dickson dropped the cigarette butt to the floor and ground it out with his heel. 'I'll impress on him the ah, novelty of the situation facing us.'

'I'd be obliged. What about the Yanks?'

'The phone cables are running red hot. Sooner rather than later, we're going to have to tell the CIA. They'll have satellite photographs within a day or so, and be asking us some very pointed questions.'

'Fortunately, that's not my problem,' said Thacker, 'though I don't envy the person who has to tell them one of their airliners has been brought down by an English country house.'

He walked back behind his table, and extinguished the light on the projector. He cleared his throat, set his cap back on his head, and asked: 'Right. Has anyone got any questions? Sensible ones that I might be able to answer.'

# 2

They were all volunteers, Thacker had made sure of that – genuine volunteers, too, not the kind of line up where some vindictive bastard of a senior officer picks the soldiers who've clocked up the most charges.

They'd come to him, one by one, and said that they were scared but they'd do it. Thacker would nod grimly and mutter, 'Good man', and write a name down on his clipboard. Those too scared simply didn't show. No blame attached. Every time Thacker looked down the sweep of the hill to the red-brick pile surrounded by nothing but ash and decay, he felt like running for home, too.

He checked his equipment one more time. Full NBC suit. Air-tight save for the heavy respirator strapped hard onto his face.

Thacker had been exposed to all the known war gasses, and many of the biological weapons, in a suit just like this one. He'd survived. He was immune to anthrax and two strains of smallpox. The bubonic plague was treatable with a simple course of antibiotics.

Rifle. Bayonet. Spare clips of ammunition. He had his handgun as well, but he wanted something with a little more punch. Geiger-Muller tube. He turned it on, listened to it crackle away like someone was folding thick brown paper, then off again. There was a dosimeter badge on his webbing. Gas detector. Such a shame there was no biological equivalent. Torch. Night vision goggles he could hold over his respirator eyepieces.

Radio. And a mobile phone for emergencies. Grenades. Standard issue NATO fragmentation, and the not-so standard issue phosphor bombs.

The equipment was piled on a small plastic sled, the sort kids used for two days each year when it became snowy enough, and spent the other three hundred and sixty three days wishing for winter. Being the army, the sled was dark green and ten times more expensive than the red versions sold in the shops.

The instruments he pulled weren't necessarily heavy, but bulky. Others in the squad had to lug a portable laboratory, complete with blowtorch to seal off glass sample vials. There was a big gas chromatograph in the back of the Warrior armoured car, but it was on wheels and would be out and his men in at the first sign of trouble.

The car had a thirty millimetre cannon and smoke launchers, and the inner compartment had been specially modified to be airtight.

Thacker still didn't know who, or what, if anything, he was supposed to be fighting. After all those years of hanging around a chemical weapons establishment, he felt more like a scientist – at least a competent technician – than a soldier.

Only the once had he ever had to put his training to use. That had been a long time ago, and absolutely no one knew about it. Perhaps Dickson did, but Thacker couldn't ask him.

The sun was coming up. The shapes in the valley were becoming distinct: the dead hands of leafless trees, the rotten walls of buildings. Long shadows were forming across the dust and ash of the estate. It was as dead as it was yesterday.

Thacker pulled his sled to the start of the long gravel drive, and the guards pulled the coil of razor wire aside, taking exaggerated care that the barbs didn't puncture their own suits.

Behind him he could hear the rustling and rasping of clothing and plastic on stone. The engine of the Warrior started up, a great roar of diesel, and he felt just a little more confident.

When they were all through the gap, and the wire barricade replaced, he motioned for his men to fan out in an arrow shape, the point on the driveway, and the armoured car just a little behind. He started forward, one hand on his rifle, one on his sled rope. Where the soldiers to his left and right walked on what had been, eighty years ago, grass, little clouds of matter stirred up and clung to their legs, coating everything in a fine layer of bone-dry powder.

His radio man waved. He wasn't pulling a sled, but had a high-powered satellite transmitter strapped to his back. Thacker went over, treading for the first time off the road. It felt like snow under his boots: a soft collapsing compaction that almost squeaked under each footfall.

'What is it?' shouted Thacker through his respirator.

'I'm getting interference. Nothing specific: white noise across most of the radio spectrum. There's a rough peak around fourteen megahertz, but there's no transmission.'

'Is it significant?'

'No idea, sir. It's slap-bang in the short wave band, which could foul up our own handsets, but I can still contact Comms. Just thought you ought to know.'

Thacker nodded. Caution was good. 'Tell me if it starts to affect our ability to talk to base. Otherwise, keep an eye on it.'

It was the first strange thing that morning, and it

wasn't too bad. Thacker assumed his position at the head of the arrow, and taking up his sled, started walking again.

It was, according to the maps, just over half a mile to the hall from the gates. Not far in anyone's terms. Thacker could run it in less than three minutes, in normal conditions. Conditions were far from normal, but he felt he could break a record or two if he had to.

He was two hundred yards in, when his rifle twisted in his hand like it had suddenly come alive. He had no idea what was happening, but knew he didn't like it. He dropped the sled rope and brought the weapon up in one quick snap. The gun wouldn't point straight, and he stumbled back. Now he had control of it.

The other eight men had all crouched down and were scanning the empty land for targets.

Thacker braced the gun butt against his shoulder and inched forward. He could feel the pressure against the barrel that was turning it away. He pushed back against the force and felt it slip aside the other way.

When he had been a child, he had been fascinated by magnets, especially when he'd try to bring two of the same polarity together. They would squirm in his fingers, resisting all the more the closer they came.

It was like that now. His gun was being repelled by an invisible force. Thacker backed off again, and bent down to scoop up a handful of dusty gravel in his gloved hand.

Then with a high throw, he scattered the dirt into the air, and watched the curtain of debris stick in mid-air and slide gently to the ground.

'Now how about that,' he said under his breath. To the soldier charged with carrying the video camera, he called, 'Did you get that?'

The private stood on his shaking legs and picked up

the discarded camera. He was still trying to aim his rifle.

'Should I do that again?' asked Thacker.

'I'd rather you didn't, sir.'

'Any change in any of the readings: radiation?'

'Background only, sir.'

'Right.' Thacker would have scrubbed his chin with the fleshy part of his thumb, but he didn't have access to either. He kicked his heel against the ground, then shot the air in front of him.

The bullet, perfectly formed and still glowing from the propellant, span slowly in the air. He had time to lower his gun and inspect it closely before it started to fall to the ground.

'The question is, can anything get out?'

His radio squawked, and he turned away to answer it. 'Thacker. Over.'

'Dickson. Sorry I'm late. Bloody politicians and all that. You shooting pheasants?' Pause. 'Over.'

'How much of this can you see?'

'I've a very large set of binoculars. I'm also getting a feed from a helicopter outside the perimeter.'

'Whatever you do, don't send it in. If it runs into what we've just run into, you'll lose it.'

'Talk to me, Major. Tell me something I can use.'

'For the want of a better word, it's a force-field. Shape unknown, though it's probably centred on the house. It deflects metallic and non-metallic objects, and stops a bullet dead in its tracks.'

Dickson digested the news. 'You've got surveying equipment down there, yes? Map the outer edge. There may be a way through.'

Thacker's small band of soldiers were unconsciously backing away towards the main gate. They were already level with the armoured car. He had to take control, give them something to do rather than contemplate the impossible. Too much thinking was bad for squaddies.

'I'll get back to you. Over and out.'

He called them together, close in, like a scrum, their heads almost touching. He told them what he wanted them to do, and told them to go and do it. That bought him some time. When the soldiers had dispersed to their tasks, he hefted the radio again.

'Dickson?'

'Loud and clear, Major.'

'That matter we were talking about last night. Did you get anywhere?'

'I'm afraid I'll have to talk in circumlocutions. Careless talk and all that. I mentioned it to my superiors. They are a little, how can I put it, squeamish about the idea.'

'Why does that not surprise me? Dickson, press them. Press them hard. Tell them I'm crapping in my hermetically-sealed pants out here, and I'd breathe a lot easier if I knew it wasn't all riding on me.'

'What happened to the rufty-tufty army boy, Thacker?'

'This house, this bloody force-field, the fact that everything here is dead, dead, dead, and we have no explanations for anything. Do it, Dickson. Make them see sense.'

'I'll do my best. They, and not us, have command. Unless you're going to organise a putsch. Tell me about this invisible wall.'

'I'm hoping that as nothing can get in, nothing can get out. I'd bet a pound to a penny that this is what brought down the plane. But I don't think the force-field's stable. It's contracting back to its source, somewhere in the main building. It started off at the perimeter, and it's been retreating ever since. I'll know for sure when the surveying's done, and how long we have before the field goes to zero.'

'What happens then?'

'Damn you, Dickson. I was hoping you were going to tell me.'

'We have to know before it happens.'

'Then tell me how to get through the field. Things inside appear to be able to come out: we've dead grass and dead trees to prove that point. But a moving object … I have an idea. Speak to you in five minutes.'

Thacker took a slim gas probe from his sled and advanced on the field. He felt he had taken a step further than he ought to have done. He checked with the first of the surveying poles spiking the ground. It was true. He was a foot closer to the house than previously.

He held out the probe, and tried to slide it through the air in front of him. It stopped, was pushed away. He tried again, slower this time. It was like pushing an elephant with a matchstick. But the probe eased in. When he let go, the probe stayed, suspended, and didn't fall. He tried to pull it back, and it resolutely refused to come until he exacted the same sort of Zen-like control on his hand as he had when inserting the probe.

He went back to the sled. 'Dickson.'

'Here.'

'I think I can get in. It's not a question of hitting it so hard that it breaks, it's going so slowly that it doesn't think you're moving at all. There's some sort of threshold speed, no more than half an inch a second. The field is definitely contracting, so I'm rather assuming that I can get permission to attempt a breach.'

'What do you need?'

'Apart from the nerves of steel I haven't got? A wheeled trolley and precision hydraulic ram. There should be some engineering works in Oxford – the

Cowley car plant should have what we want.'

'I'm on to it. Over and out.'

Thacker watched his men slowly return. The grey ash near the force-field was festooned with red and white surveying poles. They had their readings, and could now make an estimate of how long they had before …

Before what? Ragnorok? Armageddon? Or nothing more than a damp squib of nothing.

Thacker was beyond guessing. He pulled his troops out, the Warrior covering their retreat with its cannon.


Everyone had to go through decontamination, despite the fact that they'd detected nothing. It was good practice, but nothing more. He inspected the men who'd gone in with him, thanked them for their duty, and dismissed them. They wandered away as if shell-shocked.

Thacker could still smell and taste the rubber of his respirator. Rank had its privileges, and he commandeered a cup of tea. He found himself back in the marquee he had used for the briefing. His notes were still at the front, now neatly boxed away in a lockable trunk. He nodded to the guard.

'Do you want me to wait outside, sir?'

'I imagine that would probably be best. Get yourself to the mess. I'll shoot any spies myself.' He patted his sidearm.

He sat at the trestle table and fished out the key from the string around his neck. The padlock was old and stiff. He ought to oil it, or better still, get a modern strongbox with a modern lock, not a nineteen twenties effort that could be jemmied off in seconds.

He dug out Middleton's report again, and wondered what he was missing. He'd read it over and over, virtually memorised it verbatim. Yet it gave him no clue as to what had happened to the five miles of countryside around Henbury Hall.

He put the paper to one side and took out the maps, and compared them to the sketches and figures that his detachment had made. The global positioning system had made quick, accurate surveying something so simple that even a private could manage it.

Thacker plotted out the details as accurately as his propelling pencil would allow. Then he did the sums in the margins. He looked at his watch, and added the time to his precise, spidery maths.

Dickson came striding back in, cigarette in his mouth and a clipboard in his hand. He slapped the clipboard down in front of Thacker.

'That do?' he said out of the corner of his mouth.

Thacker looked at the Ford receipt, and the technical details of the apparatus Dickson had commandeered.

'Looks fine. You know what I have in mind?'

'A couple of engineers are bolting it all together, then they need to test it. Should be ready to go in an hour.'

'Thank you. Makes a difference, not having to explain everything five times.' He grinned and drank some tea.

Dickson tugged hard on his cigarette, the end burning fiercely for a few seconds. 'What's your estimate?'

'That we have ten hours, plus or minus an hour, until the field contracts to zero. The rate of retreat is relatively constant, but trying to measure the edge of something you can't see and that is continually moving is a little tricky. Hence the error.' Thacker shuffled the aerial photograph to the top. 'More importantly, the field is centred in the west wing of the house.'

'Is that significant?' Dickson leaned over and expelled a cloud of smoke. Thacker coughed and waved it away.

'Emily Foster was quite clear. Everyone lived in the east wing.'

'And?'

'Perhaps there was something going on that neither she nor Middleton knew about.'

'Like what? We can hardly credit some secret government experiment. I'd know about it.'

'Well, something made a large country estate disappear into thin air.' Thacker threw his pencil down in annoyance. 'It wasn't David Copperfield. Or even Houdini.'

'This is the point,' said Dickson, lighting a new cigarette from the stub of the old one. 'You can't give me anything as a credible threat, yet you want authorisation to nuke half of Oxfordshire.'

Thacker regarded the Ministry man coolly. 'Shout a bit louder. I don't think they heard you in Whitehall.'

'I apologise. I'm a bit spooked.'

'Aren't we all? I barely held that lot together down there. I genuinely thought they'd turn and run at one point. Felt like it myself.' Thacker played with the dregs of his drink and swilled them down. 'It's all very strange.'

'So why not just wait ten hours?' asked Dickson. 'Wait until the field has contracted to zero and then just stroll in?'

'Because there might be nothing left to see by then. I want to get in there and find out before we maybe lose whatever is in there. Put it down to scientific curiosity.'

'What are you taking in with you?'

'The bare minimum. I'm not going to mount a full expedition. Me and a weapon, if I can get away with that. I expect I'll have to take a radio in, but a pound to a penny it won't work.' Thacker stood up and manhandled the whiteboard from its stand, pocketing one of the pens that fell to the floor. 'This'll have to do instead, unless you know sign language.'

'I'm only fluent in Russian.'

'Pity. My daughter's deaf, did you know?'

'I'm sure I read it in your file. Amongst other things.' Dickson finished his cigarette, and extinguished the butt under his heel.

'Ah,' said Thacker. 'So you know about that as well.'

'Military Cross. Shame you can't tell your family about it. They'd be very proud.'

'I trust they'd be proud of me if I was working on the bins.' He hefted the whiteboard, and started for the tent flap. 'Dickson, I don't mean to needle you. It's the situation.'

Dickson nodded, and patted his pockets for his lighter. 'Stop being so bloody reasonable, man.'

They marched down the main drive in front of the Warrior, with the Heath Robinson arrangement Thacker was going to use installed inside. A squaddie had taken point, a surveying pole extended out like a pike, looking for the start of the force-field.

Thacker carried a cage of white mice and a pressurised cylinder of halon.

Fifty yards on from the last surveying point, the man on point came to an abrupt halt, and held up his hand.

'Right,' called Thacker, 'let's unload. Time is fleeting.'

The other soldiers heaved the contraption out of the armoured car and carried it as close to the house as they could. It was a hydraulic car-ramp jack on a carriage. Bolted to the moving end of the jack was a man-sized wheeled board that bore a faded Ford logo. Slung under the carriage was a motor and a modified hydraulic pump.

It would move at the achingly low speeds required to pierce the barrier.

But first, Thacker was going to send etherised mice through. And to anyone who would have argued, he would have insisted that of course he was more important than a couple of bloody rodents.

He put the cage on the very front of the trolley and gaffer-taped it down. The mice scampered around, sniffing the strange air full of odour.

'Right, edge it forward.'

The men pushed the carriage until the trolley was abutting the field.

'Gentlemen, start your engines.'

At the roar of the two-stroke, the mice dived for cover. Thacker could see their little noses twitch, trembling the sawdust. He gave them a blast of anaesthetic, and the twitching stopped.

He stood, and motioned for them to start the pump. As he watched, the cage started to buckle.

'Slower! You're going too fast.'

The needle valve on the hydraulics was closed even tighter. Thacker got back down on his hands and knees. The cage was keeping its shape. The trolley wheels were going round, their motion barely perceptible.

'Steady.'

After a minute of pushing, Thacker called a halt. The cage was inside, intact. He couldn't see the mice.

'Do you want me to bring the cage back?'

'Not yet. Wait.'

At first he thought it was his eyes, blurring with tears through the strain of looking too intently. Then he realised that the blurs were the mice moving about their tiny world. They seemed like fat white ghosts, sliding about behind the thin wire bars. Thacker blinked hard. He could just about make out features: a whisker drawn into a solid plane; a pink nose a drawn out smudge. Then he noticed the cage itself seemed strangely extended, stretched out through the force-field.

'Okay, wind it back in. Slowly.'

The mice were alive inside the area of influence. If they made it back out again, he'd be strapping himself to the board in a few minutes, and praying that nothing went wrong.

# 3

He took his knife and cut himself free. His hands were trembling, out of fear, out of cold. He had to make especially sure that he was slicing the tape that had held him still, and not the suit that could well be keeping him alive.

He cut by his neck, and sat up. He twisted around on the wheeled board and looked back through the force-field to the life beyond. There was nothing to see. The estate extended on, all grey grass and skeletal trees. The end of the board stretched away, and grew indistinct.

Everything was wrong, and Thacker knew it, even as he freed his legs from the last bindings. The whiteboard was under him. He drew two letters on it, 'OK', and left it in the dust. He had to hurry, really hurry. It had occurred to him, far too late to do anything about it, that time moved differently inside the field. Even allowing for a year to have passed for Henbury Hall, he had about five minutes real time before …

Before what? He still didn't know. He had to find out. He picked up his rifle and feeling less brave than at any time in his life, he started jogging towards the buildings.

There was a torch strapped to the top of his weapon. He tried it. The beam was momentarily bright, then it just faded away to a pale glimmer. Thacker hit the torch once, twice, and the glow died.

It was cold and dark. He knew where the sun should be in the sky, and it just wasn't there anymore. There was a faint greyness to the sky, enough to see shapes, too little to see detail. It would have to do.

As he ran, he kicked up spurts of dust that hung in the air like fog.

The stables were off to his left, along with the workshop. Ahead of him was the hall itself, a fat shadow with tall chimneys like teeth. It was only gothic revival architecture, but in the gloom it looked plain evil.

Thacker made it to the front door, a heavy wooden portal studded with iron nails. The door was ajar, the latch operated by the heavy ring seemingly frozen in the open position.

He put his shoulder to it. The hinges creaked like gunshots, and he immediately desisted. There was no one there. They'd all gone, all been lost, all he'd find were corpses. He pushed again, and slowly, reluctantly, the door crawled open. He took a few moments at the threshold for his eyes to adjust, then raised his rifle and stepped in.

He listened very carefully. The only sound was his own heart. The entrance hall was on a grand scale, with a staircase directly ahead of him leading up to a balcony that led both left – west – and right – east. According to Emily Foster's testimony, the household lived in the east wing. The phenomenon was centred on the other side of the house.

West it was, then. He climbed the stairs two at a time, glancing behind him every so often at the pale rectangle of the open front door. How nice it would be to just cut and run, except the retreating field would have left his body board behind like the retreating tide. There was only one way out now.

He was on the landing. The doors everywhere were open, gaping mouths of darkness that led into the rooms beyond. The world beyond the windows was barely visible. He turned, checked his back again, and went through into the west wing of the house.

A carpet, a runner that didn't stretch to the edges of the corridor, seemed to crumble with each step he took. The passage stretched almost the whole length of the wing. There were lots of doors, all open, and the occasional table with a vase of sticks and paintings too dark to determine the subject matter. And something underfoot, like stones. He checked above him for fallen plaster, but found none.

He worked his way down, checking each room with a kick and a crouch and a pan of his rifle sights. By the time he reached the last room, his nerves were in shreds and gripping his rifle would have been impossible if not for his rubber gauntlets: his whole body was swimming with cold sweat.

This room was different. Every other room had been bare, stripped out: no curtains or carpets or furniture. This at least had a writing desk and a chair, and in the corner, a naked iron bedstead. He had to assume it was significant. There was also another door in the west wall. Open, of course.

He used the wall for cover, noting briefly that there were papers, a notebook perhaps, on the desk. He'd come back for those later. His back pressed against the plasterwork, he edged around the room. How much time did he have, if any at all? He stood next to the door frame, and then turned, kicked and crouched.

There it was. It had to be the reason. Thacker looked all around the room, checking the shadows for movement, then moved closer.

It was just taller than he, and as broad at the base as it was high, a brass cone knotted with pipes and coils that danced through and out without meaning. Its surface was hammered with shapes, strangely familiar yet utterly alien. There was a control panel of sorts, too, with heavy levers.

And it was humming with power.

He circled it twice, and realised that there were no cables to trip over. Poor on history, he wasn't sure whether houses in 1919 had electricity, and how it could have been hooked up to the National Grid for the past eighty years. He reached out and touched it. He could feel a soft vibration in his palm.

The thing itself was alive.

He backed out through the door, reluctant to turn his back on it, and collided with the desk. He jumped, cursed himself for being stupid and cowardly, and bent to retrieve some of the papers that had fallen to the floor.

They were thick with writing, and Thacker could barely make out the fine, copperplate script. But there were diagrams, more drawings of symbols – abstract designs, stylised people and birds – and a huge folded sheet like a map, except that it was a wiring diagram the likes of which he had never seen.

He looked again at the pictures. They seemed Egyptian: hieroglyphs.

Then two things: he realised that it was growing lighter outside, and there was a creak of floorboards in the corridor. He'd been standing there, with his back to the door. He dropped to his knee and aimed. Something moved, and was gone. Footsteps, running.

He turned the corner in time to see nothing more than a shadow at the far end of the corridor. Distracted by the sight of the light coming in from the windows, he missed his chance to call out a warning, or even snap off a shot.

Sunlight streamed across the blasted parkland turned

grey, and beyond he could see green trees and fields of unripe wheat. There was blue sky. The force-field had collapsed, and he hadn't even noticed.

Now, when his radio would work, he didn't have it. He had to assume that soldiers would now be coming down the main drive, fanning out through the building, and that he could quite easily be shot by someone on his own side. Very easily, assuming they were as spooked as he was.

He didn't run. He stalked. Whoever – whatever – he was chasing would know the hall intimately. Every hiding place, every twist and turn, every concealed passageway. Thacker had trained for this; not recently, but often enough in the past for the training to have stuck. Weapon out in front, finger on the trigger, and slowly.

He gained the balcony overlooking the entrance, and barely recognised it. The light, previously denied, showed plain wooden panelling, yellowing whitewash walls and dusty boards. Nothing to be scared of, really.

Coming down the stairs, he listened. Outside, he could hear in the distance the sound of a large engine revving. The Warrior would be advancing, with a column of soldiers behind it. Inside, there was the scraping of something heavy across the floor, dragged in short steps. He quickened his pace, crossed the entrance hall, and touched one of the big double doors.

He caught a glimpse of a huge banqueting room, big leaded windows, massive stone fireplace, and a towering, teetering bonfire of broken wood in the very centre of the space. In the corner was an upturned table, and on top of the edge was the barrel of a shotgun aimed at him.

As he stepped back, the gun fired, booming in the

confined space. The door quivered as buckshot punctured the dense wood. He was through the door, rolling, looking for cover, even as he fired a burst of three into the corner. The shotgun boomed again. Plaster dust trailed the chalk-white chunks of wall as they arced to the floor.

Thacker had put the wood-pile between him and the table. He kept it in line as he moved cautiously forward. A shot hit the fireplace off to his right. Sharp shards of stone zipped through the air. Several hit Thacker, hard enough to hurt, not enough to cut his suit. That hadn't been a shot gun; a rifle instead.

He cleared his throat.

'My name is Major Thacker, of the British Army. You have one chance to lay down your weapons and come out. I have reinforcements arriving as I speak, and we will use deadly force without hesitation. Surrender now.'

There were more noises outside, feet on gravel, the front door being charged aside. Any second now, someone was going to come barging through behind him, straight into the line of fire. Thacker aimed at the windows and shot them out.

Victorian glass shattered in a waterfall of crystal that caught the sunlight just so. The cannon on the armoured car returned fire, and everything that was still standing disintegrated, along with most of the back wall. When the turret had finished its rake, there was silence for a moment, only punctuated by the sound of falling masonry.

Thacker looked at the door, saw the facemask of a respirator looking in at him. He raised two fingers, pointed to the corner of the room. He got a thumbs-up sign in return and the instruction to cover his face.

Three black disks skidded across the floor, and as

Thacker pressed his hands over his ears and screwed his eyes tight shut, there was an echoing explosion of light and sound.

Abruptly, there were soldiers pouring into the room, firing staccato bursts at the corner, running forward, lying down, covering their comrades as they leap-frogged over them and gained more ground.

Thacker was up and running, too, outflanking the tabletop and gaining a clear shot behind it.

'Hold your fire!' he shouted. Some heard him. Others, intent on reducing the table to matchwood, carried on.

'Cease fire!' It was a bellow, muffled by his respirator, but he moved forward as well. Fingers left triggers, and the last shellcase span to a stop.

He enunciated as clearly as he could.

'Put your weapons down now, and stand up.'

Two men, pale and filthy, clambered to their feet. Rather one of them did, and helped the other up. This second man was missing a leg.

'Stand down, everyone. Shooting's over.' He beckoned to the men. 'Come on, out. Slowly does it.'

They shuffled out. Their clothes were ragged, torn. Their cheeks were concave and their eyes were white and bulging. They were terrified of him.

'Are you Robert Henbury?'

At this, the one-legged man started to cry. He leaned all the harder against the other man and buried his head in his chest.

'And you are?'

'Adams,' he said, in a voice not used to speaking.

'George Adams?'

'Yes.' He hesitated. 'Are you human?'

The question sent a thrill of fright down Thacker's spine.

'I was last time I looked. My name's Thacker. I'm a Major in the British Army. Welcome back, gentlemen.'

Adams and Henbury were just about able to walk, but Thacker wouldn't let them. He called for stretchers and told the men to sit and wait.

He studied them as they slumped on the floor, clinging to each other like frightened children. They looked quite mad: hair grown unchecked and hacked inexpertly back when it had got in the way, beards ragged in the same unkempt way, and that hollow-cheeked, wide-eyed unblinking stare they both had as if they expected something blasphemous to appear at a moment's notice. Their fingers were bandaged and bloody, their nails cracked and yellow. The clothes they wore were like the carpets, threadbare and shedding matter in clouds of dust.

Thacker's own appearance couldn't help either, he realised. Adams and Henbury disappeared in 1919. As far as he could tell, they hadn't aged a jot. Even allowing for the terrible air of decay that hung about them, they hadn't experienced so much as a single year. Now they were confronted with camouflaged monsters with a boggling array of weaponry – straight out of an HG Wells novel. Chalk one up to Einstein and the theory of relativity.

So Thacker was trying to limit the strangeness these two travellers could see. The radios, they'd probably recognise as telephones without wires, and surmise that Marconi's little discovery had got a little smaller. The Warrior? They'd had tanks at Cambrai. Even the NBC suit he wore was just a few decades later on from gas masks and urine-soaked cloth wound around the head.

He'd save the medical, digital and genetic revolutions

for later, not to mention that the War to end all Wars had been followed by a century of shocking brutality on and off the battlefield.

The stretchers and their bearers arrived, suited up in white coveralls with big red crosses front and back. Something else they'd recognise.

'Get on,' said Thacker, 'and we'll give you a lift to decontamination. It'll be undignified, and it may even hurt, but after that we can get a doctor to take a look at you.'

Neither Adams nor Henbury moved.

'Yes, I will force you. You can't stay here, and you really have no choice but to do what we tell you.' Thacker stepped between Adams and the resting shotgun, and pointed his rifle nowhere in particular. 'I think you could both do with a shower, a shave and a hot meal. What do you say?'

Adams was the first to move. He got up to a crouching position and put his shoulder under Henbury's arm. One of the orderlies went to help, and Henbury flinched as if he'd been electrocuted. Adams steadied him, and the orderly made another attempt at assistance.

This time, reluctantly, Henbury leaned on him as well, and together they lowered the one-legged man to the plastic stretcher. Adams lay on his, and they were hoisted aloft with surprising ease. Or not so surprising. There was more meat on a scarecrow.

Both were carried away out of the hall and into the blinding sunshine, Thacker following at a discreet distance. He was caught by one of his squad brandishing a radio handset.

'It's Mr. Dickson, sir.'

Thacker sighed and took the radio, pressing the earpiece hard against the side of his head.

'Thacker? Two casualties?'

'Yes. Rather a pleasant surprise. Lord Robert Henbury and George Adams. I suppose we should call them survivors rather than casualties, but we're treating them as such.'

'What shape are they in?'

'Emaciated. And if not all mad, at least half mad. They tried to kill me when they saw me the first time, but lucid enough not to try it twice. I've sent them for full decontamination, and we'll keep them in isolation until we're certain their blood is clear.'

'How old are they?'

'Ah. Not really any older than when they left. Bit of a mystery, that one. Time moved differently inside the field.' Thacker looked around. Because of the respirator, he was shouting his replies, and there were things he didn't want broadcast. 'I'm going to order the main building sealed. There's something inside that I don't want touched by anyone less than an expert.'

'Are you being enigmatic?'

'Just for the moment. I'm coming back to the basecamp now, and get out of this damnable suit. And I need to make sure Henbury and Adams are treated properly, not as objects of curiosity or plain-old lab rats. I think they've been through more than enough. Adams asked me if I was human.'

'Did he? Why did he do that?'

'I have absolutely no idea at all. I rather assumed it was the get-up I'm wearing. Although it did strike me as a little odd.'

Dickson was silent for a while, so long that Thacker assumed that the connection had been cut. He was just handing the radio back when it squawked again.

'Thacker? Thacker?'

'I'm still here.'

'We might have a problem.'

'Over and above the ones we already have?'

'Yes. Imagine you're on guard duty. Someone approaches and asks you if you're British.'

'And …'

'They could be asking you because they're British, too, and they're your friend.'

Thacker got the point. 'And they could be asking because they're not, and they want to kill you.' He looked up the hill to where the stretcher party were. They had almost reached the main gates. 'Get a squad together and meet me at decontamination.' He thrust the radio into the squaddies' chest. 'No one goes in or out of that building until I say so. Check for external doors and post a double-guard on every last one.'

He started running, hating how the suit slowed him down and made him awkward.

# 4

He watched Henbury and Adams very carefully after that. The seed had been planted in his mind, and he was sure he would never look at them in the same way again. That was Dickson's skill as a civil servant – to brush aside the seemingly obvious to reveal an insidious menace that could ruin everything. That was how he worked, warping trusting souls into suspicious minds. Thacker could only assume that Dickson thought it kept the country safe, the price of freedom being eternal vigilance.

All Thacker knew was that tiny actions now carried enormous significance. The way they continually picked at the all-in-one coveralls given to them after their clothes had been bagged as high-grade biological waste and shipped post haste to Porton Down. The way they ate, like starved dogs wary of another random kicking. The way they examined every item that looked new and unusual, from the guns the soldiers carried to the nylon rope fixing the tent down.

Most of all, the way they talked to each other in low, urgent whispers, using only a pared-down version of English, as if the very words they used were rationed.

It was now entirely Dickson's show. Somewhere along the line it had turned into an MI5 operation. Thacker was just there to assist, and shoot something or someone if it was deemed necessary.

But rather than freezing him out, Dickson took him into his confidence. Thacker was one of the few people on site who had a security clearance as high as he did.

Just before they entered the isolation tent, they put on the gauze masks used by surgeons. Henbury and Adams had missed eighty years of pandemics, and in their weakened state, a common cold could carry them off. Dickson was carrying a small tape recorder in his hand.

Thacker let Dickson go first. He followed closely behind, his hand resting on his webbing belt, just behind his sidearm. Henbury looked up from his scraped clean plate and backed away fractionally.

Dickson took a chair opposite. Thacker declined to sit, and stood at ease slightly behind and to the right. It afforded him a clear shot.

'Is the food all right?' asked Dickson.

Henbury dropped his spoon onto the crockery. 'Not enough salt.'

'Apparently too much salt gives you hypertension.' When his comment was met by blank incomprehension, he added: 'High blood pressure. Bad for the heart.'

'Who are you?' grunted Adams, pugnacious and wiry. Once, he'd been solidly built, muscle on his yeoman's frame. Now he was gaunt, but still bellicose.

'My name's Dickson. I'm part of the, er, Secret Service. Major Thacker, you met in the hall. He's regular army, like you were.' Dickson placed the tape recorder on the table between them. 'Do you know what that is?'

Henbury started to reach forward, and Adams caught his wrist. They looked at each other, and after a book's worth of unspoken words, put their hands back in their laps.

'It's a tape recorder,' said Dickson, faintly annoyed. 'It records sound waves on magnetic tape, which can be played back over and over again. I want to sit it on the table between us so that it can record this and subsequent interviews. It's just a machine.' He pressed the record button with his thumb and laid the whirring thing down. 'Would you both like to state your names and your dates of birth?'

'No,' said Henbury.

'This is getting stale already. We can keep you here for as long as we want. Forever, in fact. We can do to you whatever we want, up to and including killing you, if we think it'll serve the national interest. Neither of you legally exist, and until we get some answers from you, you won't be legally dead, either.'

Thacker frowned, and cleared his throat. The surgeon's mask was a minor irritation compared with the full army respirator. 'You both scare us. You've been somewhere unimaginable, and now you've returned. It's Mr Dickson's job to make sure you, or anything else that might have come with you, doesn't pose a threat to the country. If you cooperate with us now, we can reach an informed decision, and sooner rather than later.'

Henbury seemed to slump even further back in his seat. 'What's your job, then?'

'To make sure Dickson gets what he wants from you. Look, this isn't going to be some good cop, bad cop shtick.'

Dickson smiled. 'Shall we start again? Names, please.'

There was silence, then Henbury's quiet, defeated voice: 'Robert Arthur Geoffrey Leslie Henbury, born eighteenth of February, 1893. Now you, Adams.'

Adams grunted, then said: 'George James Adams, twenty-first of April, 1886.'

'Thank you, gentlemen. For the record, I'm handing to Robert Henbury the front page of today's *Times*.' Dickson shook the broadsheet out and pushed it across the table.

Henbury took it warily. His first reaction was to

dismiss it. 'This isn't *The Times*.'

'Not as you recognise it. It's still *The Times*. Still printed in London.'

Henbury flattened out a crease with the palm of his hand. Adams, despite himself, leaned over.

'Who are these people? I've never heard of any of them.' Henbury was bewildered, and then he followed Adams' quaking finger to the dateline at the top of the page.

'It's a lie. A trick. You're trying to trick us!' Adams was on his feet, unsteady, fingers gripping the tabletop.

Thacker's fingers wandered to the butt of his pistol. 'You've travelled, not in space but in time. Eighty years into the future. Now you're here, and we have to deal with this whole extraordinary situation. Will you tell us where you've been, and what happened to you while you were there? If you like, you can start by explaining what that contraption is on the first floor of the west wing.'

Both men were too agitated to continue. Henbury crumpled the news sheet in his fist and gaped at Dickson, then at Thacker, and back again. Adams started to swear, using damn and blast and bloody like they were going out of fashion.

'We'll try again in the morning,' said Dickson, and clicked the tape recorder off.


Outside, Dickson searched furiously for a cigarette, and didn't stop his frenetic activity until the first rush of smoke had been sucked deep into his lungs.

'That went well,' said Thacker.

'Bollocks it did. We both lost our rag. Too eager to prove that Little Lord Henbury and his sidekick are either homicidal lunatics or impostors from the ninth dimension bent on world domination.'

'You know, you have a turn of phrase that's almost poetic.'

Dickson laughed. 'And you're too phlegmatic.'

'When I was down in that house, I was crapping myself every step of the way.'

'Yes, but you did the job. Henbury should recognise your type: the Empire was built on people like you.' Dickson chain-lit another cigarette and stubbed out the old one on a tent pole.

Thacker flipped off his face mask. 'Do you want to take a look at the device in the house? There's still enough light left.'

'Don't want to go poking around in the dark? Can't blame you. Sure, why not. Do I have to wear that ridiculous NBC suit?'

'Not if you don't mind some rogue pathogen coagulating your blood in an instant, or rupturing every cell in your body.' Thacker scratched his ear. 'We've got things like that back in the lab, all safely locked up.'

Dickson pursed his lips. His cigarette nodded up and down. 'They've some civvy getup at the portable lab. I'll borrow one of those.'

They met back at the main gate, Thacker in his green coveralls and respirator, Dickson in his shiny white spaceman's suit and plastic-fronted helmet.

'I suppose getting a lift's out of the question?' asked Dickson.

'It's not far,' said Thacker, and started walking. Again, he'd traded his sidearm for a rifle.

They crunched along the gravel drive, and watched as zephyrs of wind caught the grey ash and sent it drifting across the dead ground.

'Wind's picking up,' said Dickson. 'Front coming in from the south-west. It'll be raining by tomorrow morning.'

'The dust's inert.'

'I hope that's the case. It's what I told the Prime Minister this morning. I even mentioned your name, so that when three-eyed fish start invading the capital, he knows who to blame.'

Thacker half-smiled, but the situation was too serious. They were approaching the heavy front doors, sealed with fluttering biohazard tape. The two bio-suited guards on duty were edgy. 'We're going in to take a look. Shut the doors up behind us and make certain it's us coming out. We'll give the password of the day.'

The guards stood aside, and as Thacker pushed the door inwards, they levelled their guns at the shade inside. Dickson stepped through and Thacker nodded to the soldiers.

The door clanged shut, making Dickson start.

'It's not haunted, you know.'

'Did I ever say it was? Where's this thing kept?'

'Up the stairs, left at the top.' Thacker led the way through the ageing house. 'Strange. For a building built in 1840, it should only be eighty years old according to its own internal clock. It feels so much older, older than the hundred and sixty years it really is. Like it's tired of being Henbury Hall, and wants to be a pile of rubble instead.'

Dickson, close behind, said: 'You're anthropomorphizing. Buildings don't feel.'

'I was in Germany at one of the old concentration camps. You'll never convince me that bricks and mortar can't remember.'

The corridor had changed from his last visit. All the

open doors along its length were pools of darkness, but the passage itself was basking in late sunlight. It made everything look different, but it still felt unutterably sad all the same. He breezed down its length, gaze flicking into each empty room, but there was none of the close-quarter searching of earlier.

It was odd. He had the sensation that he ought to take more care, but there was nothing concrete to pin it on.

'It's in here. Through the connecting door.'

Dickson peeked in, took in the desk and chair, and the spilled papers on the floor.

'Sorry about the mess. My fault,' said Thacker. He shuffled the closely-written sheets back into a semblance of order and put them back on the desk.

Dickson was standing at the second doorway, hands on the frame, staring at the impossible machine in front of him. 'You know what these symbols are, don't you?'

'Hieroglyphs. See? A Classics degree from Oxford does have some use.'

'Where the hell did this thing come from?' He stalked around it, much like Thacker had done. 'Before or after the disappearance?'

'I think,' said Thacker, 'this might give us some of the answers.' He held up a book covered with faded red leather. He flicked through the pages, stopping at random. 'This seems to be a diary, a journal. Everything here needs to be bagged, checked and catalogued. I found some plans earlier. At least, that's what they looked like.' He interrupted himself. 'Dickson, don't touch those.'

Dickson's hand was resting on one of the three levers. He lifted it away. 'Sorry. Curiosity.'

'Good job you're not a cat, then.' Thacker looked at the last entry in the journal and found it written in a different style. He leafed back until the handwriting changed again. He could make out 31st July, 1919. Subsequent pages were undated. He looked back at the very front. 'Jack Henbury. We've got Jack Henbury's diary, but no Jack. What do you reckon?'

Dickson was on his belly, inspecting the base of the machine. 'Can't see any power supply. It must have some sort of engine. Perhaps the force-field collapsed because it ran out of juice.'

'It's still puttering along. You can feel it humming.'

Dickson got up and brushed himself down. 'We need to get this somewhere safe. Aldermaston?'

'It's close, and they've got good containment facilities. I don't fancy trying to move it before we know how it works.'

'We may not know until we move it.'

'I, for one, am not vanishing for the next eight decades and getting back in time to see my grandchildren get married.' Thacker started to stack up all the papers and books on the desk. 'I would strongly recommend we don't shift that thing until we know a lot more about it.'

Dickson circled it again. 'It's not secure here. It makes me nervous. Though I'm rather assuming that this is the origin of the force-field, and as such is of unimaginable importance, rather than being a heap of ancient Egyptian junk.'

'The light's starting to go. If you'll carry the papers, we'll be out of here.'

'Why am I doing the donkey work?'

'Because I have the rifle, and I'd like to be able to shoot someone without asking politely for them to wait while I free my hands.'

Dickson gathered up the neat pile Thacker had made. 'Can you imagine London protected by a force-field like that? It could vanish off the map. Nothing could touch it, no bomb or missile, nothing. It could reappear a minute later and no-one inside would even notice it had happened.'

'Interesting hypothesis, Dickson. Of course, twenty million mad Londoners might just burn the whole city down in an orgy of self-destruction, if Henbury and Adams are anything to go by.'

'What do you mean?'

'That pile of wood in the banqueting hall isn't some interesting piece of modern art. It's a bonfire, and it seems I got there just in time to stop them lighting it. It says so in that journal you're carrying. Amongst other interesting things. We really do need to have a proper chat with our returnees. They didn't seem to have the energy to walk, but plenty enough to smash furniture into kindling.'

Once out of the house, Thacker shouldered his rifle and took a fair share of the paperwork.

'Look, Dickson, I don't mean be a damp squib. A force-field that'll stop cannon fire but lets air through is going to be of real interest to everyone. Especially the Pentagon. I'm sure there are more applications for it than we can dream of. But I've been inside it when it was up and running, and it felt all wrong. Clearly Henbury and Adams thought so …'

'If they are who they say they are.'

'So we'll send photographs to Emily Foster.'

'And what about on the inside?'

'CAT scan them both. If they don't die of future shock, we'll know. But you're missing the point. That machine shouldn't exist. Do you really think if the ancient Egyptians possessed such power, we wouldn't be celebrating the enthronement of Ramses the eight hundredth as Emperor of the world? Or if we had access to that sort of technology, the Great War would have lasted five minutes. Or five hundred years, depending on who had it.'

Dickson tried to scratch his nose, but had forgotten he was wearing an air-tight bubble around his head. 'Damn it, I want a cigarette.'

'And where's Jack Henbury?'

'Do you think they might have killed him?'

'If Jack had the machine first, they might well have done. I think it backfired on them. They didn't know how to work it. Instead of going away for five minutes, they were away for eighty years.'

'And the earlier deaths? The horse and the maid?'

Thacker shrugged. 'Experiments?'

'You're just guessing now, Thacker.'

'All I'm trying to do is curb your enthusiasm for something that has no right to be here and is clearly dangerous. Beware of Greeks bearing gifts.'

They walked the rest of the way in uneasy silence. At the main gate, they deposited the papers in big hazmat containers, then showered and scrubbed the outsides of their suits.

When the process had been completed, Dickson was the first to break the silence.

'I know what you're trying to do. I'm the one who's supposed to turn everything around so that it looks evil. I'm the Cassandra, warning everyone of impending doom. But think of it. A shield against everything. I could retire, and sleep easy at night knowing that nothing could go wrong even though I wasn't on watch.'

'It's not that easy,' said Thacker, unstrapping his respirator, 'and it's never that easy. Let's go and prod Henbury and Adams again. See what they have to say for themselves.'

# 5

'Right, gentlemen,' said Dickson. 'Gloves are off, and we want some straight talking from you two. I've a list of questions here, and you'll damn well answer each and every one of them.'

Adams bristled. 'Lord Henbury is a peer of the realm.'

'Which amounts to bugger all here. If you want to complain to Her Majesty – yes, I said Her Majesty – you can do so when and if I let you go.'

'Queen Elizabeth the Second,' said Thacker helpfully. 'George the Fifth's granddaughter. Succession has been maintained while you were away.'

Henbury looked pale and tired. He shifted constantly in his seat, trying to get comfortable on a backside that was lacking both fat and flesh. 'I'll trade you. Answers for some narcotic. My stump's giving me hell.'

'I can arrange that,' said Thacker. He stepped away to the tent flap and talked to the guard outside. 'It'll be here in a minute or two. In the meantime, where's Jack?'

'Jack is,' Henbury hesitated, 'probably dead. He was dying the last time we saw him.'

'And when was that?' asked Dickson.

'Time has no meaning where we've been. Everything is different there.'

'Before or after the house disappeared?'

'After.' He rubbed his too-large eyes. 'We tried to save him, just as we tried to save ourselves.'

'Robert, did you kill Jack?' Dickson spoke very quietly.

'No. I wish I had now. But it wasn't us. We did nothing. Part of the problem. Doing nothing until it was too late to do anything.'

Dickson looked up at Thacker, who returned his questioning gaze with his own. The man wasn't making any sense.

'Where did the machine come from? The one on the first floor of the west wing, far end.'

'Jack built it. He brought it from Egypt with him.'

'Archaeologist?'

'He thought so. Perhaps he was.'

'Do you know what it does?'

'It eats. That's what it does. It eats.'

'And what does it eat, Robert?'

'Everything. It consumes the vital energy from anything and kills it dead.'

Dickson tapped his pen on his clipboard. 'So why aren't you dead? And Adams?'

'How alive do we look?' snorted Adams. 'Do you think I was always like this skeleton I am now?'

'Where's Jack?'

'He's dead. He must be dead by now.'

'Where did you last see him?'

'He was …'

'Every time you stop to think, I worry that you're about to lie to me.' Dickson leaned back. 'This is not the time for lies.'

Henbury screwed his face up. 'I'm in pain.'

'I understand that. What was Jack doing when you saw him last? What makes you think he's dead?'

'He was being crucified, embedded in a metal wall. It was pulling him apart, a fraction of an inch at a time.' Henbury took gulps of air to steady himself. 'He didn't want our help, even though he was in agony. He thought they would turn him into a god, when all they were doing was sucking the very last drops of life from him. We tried to get him out, but there was no way of freeing him. He was the only one who knew how to work the machine.' And he collapsed sobbing on the tabletop, the effort of explaining too great for him.

Adams rested his hand on Henbury's shoulder and looked mutinous.

'Adams?' asked Thacker. 'Who are 'they'?'

'If we could swap places, you wouldn't believe me. So why should I waste my breath?'

'Try us. We've seen things you could only dream of.'

'They're called Ankhani. Least, that's what Jack called them. They live on a dead world at the other side of the machine. He let some of them through … to feed. That wasn't enough, so they took everything, including us.'

Dickson took out a fresh sheet of paper from his clipboard. 'These Ankhani? Do they look like us? Do they look like you?'

'No. Not like us.' Adams shuddered. 'Dull, cold things. They walk on tentacles. Big head like a half-inflated balloon. Eyes are black and hard. They die like us, mind.'

'Oh. You've killed one.' Dickson was sketching.

'More than one. Aim for the head. They burst.'

'How gratifying.' He turned the clipboard around. 'Anything like that?'

'No.' Adams snatched the board and Dickson's pen. 'Tall, upright. Two eyes on the side of the head. Ugly as sin itself. Walks on its tentacles, I said. Like legs, long like snakes. Here.'

Thacker looked over the table. If it was true, they were ghastly.

'And what do they want with us?' Dickson contemplated the monstrosity in front of him.

'Nothing. We're like cows. They use some of us for meat, and some of us for milk.'

'They're farming us?'

'If we let them. The whole world could be like the Hall.'

Thacker rubbed his chin under the surgeon's mask. 'Why didn't you tell us all this earlier? First opportunity you had?'

Adams raised himself on his hands. He leaned across the table. 'We're not bloody mad. You wouldn't have believed us then, and you don't believe us now. I can see it in his face.' He jabbed a finger at Dickson. 'He thinks we're spinning some sort of yarn, either covering up what we really did, or that we're mental with talk of monsters and doors to other worlds.'

'And what about me?' asked Thacker. 'What sort of look do I have?'

'You? You're more ready to believe. You've seen what it was like, and you can imagine it worse, trapped in your own little bubble, having every last ounce of effort drained from you until even your blood starts to run slow.'

'Sit yourself down, Mr. Adams,' said Dickson. He looked at his list. 'You were going to burn the Hall down.'

Henbury wearily raised his head. 'We were going to try one last thing. Raise the energy levels back to what they were before we were cut off. We assumed we were going to die, but any chance of escaping that hell was worth it.'

'But you never got the chance to set the fire.'

'No.'

'So how did you get back?'

'We don't know.' Henbury ground out the words. 'This is what is destroying us. We don't know why, and we are afraid. We have made not one jot of difference to that machine. It does what it does and without Jack we can't understand it.'

Thacker was distracted by the guard returning with the painkillers, a little brown bottle half-full with white pills. He heard Dickson ask: 'You said something before about a door to other worlds?'

Henbury didn't answer. He waited until Thacker had shaken out two of the pills into the palm of his hand and nudged them across the table.

'Destroy it,' he said to Thacker. 'You must have some way of annihilating matter by now, some death ray, that will make sure that thing can never be used again. If you don't destroy it, it will destroy you. Do you understand, Major?'

'I understand. It's not my call.'

'The Ankhani will come and they will take what they want and they will want to take everything.'

'I get the idea. Dickson, a word.'

As Dickson got up, Adams started cursing again. 'They don't believe us. They don't. They're not going to do anything. They're bloody well not going to do anything. They're going to try and control the blasted thing.'

Thacker closed the tent flap on the pair.

'What do you reckon?'

'Ancient Egyptian monsters sucking the life out of people? Can you imagine the Home Secretary's expression?'

'I can imagine it if they turn out to be right.'

'Thacker!'

'What reason do they have to lie? However long they've had to concoct a story, be it years or months, they ought to have come up with something better than that preposterous nonsense. And we have the unalterable fact that two days ago, Henbury Hall wasn't even on the map. So far, they've given us the only coherent explanation of what happened, fantastical though it may be.'

'Sherlock Holmes,' said Dickson.

'Sorry?'

'Sherlock Holmes. When you eliminate the impossible, whatever remains, no matter how improbable, must be the truth.'

'So is what they've said improbable or impossible?'

'I'd say it was impossible. That's what I'm going to tell my Lords and Masters.' He looked at his watch. 'I'm going to go down to London, give a briefing and get some shut-eye. I suggest you do the same. You're all washed out. I'll be back in the morning, and we can start making some plans. Like what we're going to tell the Americans, and when.'

'What's happening with the documents we brought out?'

'I'm personally taking them to the British Museum in the morning. See if they can decipher anything. It's too important to entrust to someone else.'

'I'll pack those two off to bed.'

'Don't let anyone talk to them. Or let them talk to anyone. I don't want any unilateral action. That machine is not to be touched.'

Thacker thought that last warning was directed more than a little at himself. 'I'll make sure.'


He was woken from his fitful sleep by the sound of rain on canvas. Outside, down in the valley, dust was turning to mud and sluicing away into the stream, staining it black and coating everything from there to London

Bridge with a fine layer of death.

Shapeless, nameless creatures rose up from the bed of the Thames and shambled along the Embankment, through Parliament Square and up the Mall to rot the gates of the Palace and crown themselves kings.

Then Thacker woke up for the second time. The rain was real. The rest was not.

He lay for a moment, shivering and sweating, on his camp bed, before throwing the covers to one side and dressing quickly. The floodlights outside cast shadows on the tent and gave him enough light to see by.

He strapped on his sidearm and threw on a poncho. He stepped out into the rain, the trampled grass already slick with mud, and navigated the maze of guy ropes and iron pegs to the quarantine tent where Henbury and Adams were kept.

The guards, cold and miserable, gave a half-hearted challenge, and Thacker waved them aside. He pulled the hood of his poncho back and knelt next to Henbury's bed.

The man was curled up tightly in his blankets, his face twitching with dreams.

'Henbury, wake up.'

In an instant, Henbury had gasped, shrank back, and covered his face with his hands. He peeped out through his fingers.

'It's Thacker,' he whispered. 'We need to talk.'

'Now? Yes, now, why not? The other man's gone, hasn't he?' Henbury sat up, his bed creaking.

'Dickson. He'll be back tomorrow. Listen. I'm going to ask you this once and once only. Is what you told us true?'

'Yes.'

'Oh crap.' Thacker sat on the bed next to Henbury, and regarded Adams' sleeping form. 'I still don't get this business with Jack. He brought this thing with him from Egypt, and installed it in your house, and you didn't ask any questions?'

'It wasn't like that. I didn't know what he was doing. No one did, until it was too late.'

'Everybody lived in the east wing. Except Jack. Didn't you go and see him, see what he was up to?'

Henbury lowered his head. 'When Jack came to live at the Hall, it was an act of charity. He had nowhere else to go. His father, my father's younger brother, had all but cut him off. He had an allowance that wouldn't have let him even eat in this country. Jack had been in Egypt. He came with crates of curios and artefacts. He was supposed to be writing a book about the ancients, so everything was carried to the rooms in the west wing to keep his clutter out of the way. And him.'

'You didn't get on.'

'We'd never got on. He bullied me when I was young. Until I knocked him down. Bloody *noblesse oblige*. I should have told him no.'

'Can't choose your family, can you?'

'I don't do stairs very well, with my leg missing. And … oh Christ, this is hard. I was engaged to my nurse, Emily. She started seeing Jack. I knew about it, but didn't want to think about it. Blocked it out. That was why I never went to his rooms, in case I found the two of them together. I would have had to have done something then, and it would have been all very unseemly.'

'He sounds a right bastard.' Thacker took a deep breath. 'By the way … Emily says she's sorry.'

'Pardon?'

'I saw her yesterday. She said she was sorry for hurting you.'

'Emily?' There was hope in his voice that was entirely

misplaced. 'How is she?'

'She's a hundred and five years old, Robert.' He caught the look in his eye. 'Not a good idea. You are, quite literally, from two different worlds now. It would break both your hearts. If it's any consolation at all, she missed you all her life.'

'Oh dear God, what a mess. I'm marooned in the future, and there's no way to go back.'

'We can do amazing things. We've walked on the Moon, we can talk to anyone anywhere at any time, we've cured diseases that used to kill millions. We're busy unravelling the secrets of life itself, and we still have to live one second at a time. I'm sorry, too. What are we going to do about the machine?'

Henbury wiped his nose on his sleeve and sniffed. 'Can you destroy it?'

'I don't know. Does it come apart?'

'I think it must do. Jack must have assembled it in his rooms, thinking about the number of boxes that came with him.'

'Perhaps we can take one vital part, and get rid of that.' Thacker slapped himself on the forehead. 'Dickson's got all the paperwork: diagrams, journal, everything.'

'There's always brute force.'

'I've seen it. It looks pretty solid.'

'Explosives?'

'I don't know what it was like in your day, but they don't hand out the C4 like sweeties anymore.' Thacker silently considered for a moment. 'This would cost me everything, you realise that? Dickson has dreams of a protective shield over London, and he can sell that dream to the politicians. Who wouldn't jump at it? Every city safe from missiles and bombs, skipping into a future moments after the explosion and ready to fight back.'

'It's a trap,' hissed Henbury. 'It caught Jack. Now it's caught your friend. The Ankhani will betray him, just as they betrayed Jack. You can't use it. It's theirs.'

Thacker thought hard. 'I still don't know. What if Dickson's right? I think you're mad, but are you telling me the truth?'

'You said you were only going to ask me that once.'

'So I did.'

He heard distant gunfire, echoing through the night. Rifle, fully automatic, one long burst until the magazine was empty. Adams sat up abruptly, crying out in alarm.

'Stay here,' said Thacker. Of course they would stay. They had no choice.

In the dark and the rain, the guards at the main gate were scanning the Hall and the wasteland around it with night sights.

'Who fired?'

'Someone down at the house. We've lost radio contact with the men by the kitchen door.'

'Tell everyone else to stay in position. No one's going off half-cocked.' More soldiers came up behind him, struggling to put on pieces of kit as they ran. He waited until he had collected half a dozen of them, then stepped through the barrier and started down the drive.

'Sir? What about your suit?'

'I think the creeping plague is the least of our worries. Keep trying on the radio. Tell me if you get through. Right, you lot. Double time down to the Hall. Stay together, keep your eyes peeled. If you see anything that's not human, kill it.'

# 6

They found one soldier in the shadow of the workshop wall. He was just standing, swaying slightly backwards and forwards, holding his rifle loosely in his arms. The rain fell on him as it did everyone else.

Thacker motioned for his troop to halt, then approached the man slowly. He swung a borrowed torch around until he found the man's name tag.

'Patterson? Easy son.'

He got close enough and reached out to take the gun from Patterson's unresisting grip. Slowly, the squaddie became aware of the officer, and that he wasn't wearing a respirator. He slid back his hood, and unbuckled his own rubber mask.

'It got Gary, sir.'

He pointed at three separate shapes on the ground down by the paint-peeled kitchen door.

Thacker dispatched two men to investigate. They got within a few feet, and recoiled in horror.

'Sir, he's in pieces.'

Thacker walked over, shining his torch. There was a head, together with part of the right shoulder. There was a torso, one arm attached, one arm not. And there were the legs. As if the body was a statue, and dropped to the ground.

Or perhaps frozen.

'Patterson? Did you see what did this?'

'Yes, sir.'

'Was it like an octopus that walked on its legs?'

'Yes, sir,' he replied, much to the consternation of the others.

'Did you hit it?'

'It's over by the wall, sir. I just kept on firing. I don't think there's much of it left.'

A cluster of torch beams darted to the wall, picking out the gouges in the brickwork and the dark splatter that was still dripping in sticky strands to the ground. Thacker drew his pistol, chambered the first round, and advanced.

It was there, in the angle between dirt and building. It looked like an explosion in a python's nest. There were thick, ropy tentacles coiled this way and that, joined by thin shreds of dark, rancorous flesh where its head had been. It looked very dead.

'Someone keep an eye on this.' He waited until a couple of rifles had been trained on the remains, then went to inspect the soldier.

The man's protective suit was covered in a veneer of ice, and where the body had broken, he could see layers like tree rings: clothes, skin, flesh, bone.

'What happened to him?' asked someone.

Thacker knew, but didn't tell. He looked around and saw a corporal standing nearby. 'You, man.'

'Sir?'

'Take charge. Stand right here, in a circle, facing out, away from the buildings as best you can. Patterson, reload and come with me.'

Almost in a dream-like state, Patterson wandered over, and Thacker shook him hard.

'Time for nightmares later. Right now, we've got a job to do.' Still holding onto his arm, Thacker dragged him around the front of the building to the main doors. He shouted to the pair of guards on duty there: 'Radio. Get the Warrior down here, along with every last man who can carry a weapon. Break out the anti-tank rockets and grenades.'

Patterson stumbled along behind him. 'Sir? What's happening, sir?'

'I think we're being invaded.' He deposited the man with the guards and flipped out his mobile phone. It rang and rang, and finally:

'Dickson.'

'Thacker. We have a situation.'

'Tell me.'

'Ankhani. Lost one man, sentry killed it.'

Dickson was silent while he digested the information. 'You think there's more?'

'Pound to a penny there are. I'm taking up defensive positions around the house, and if I get the chance, I'm taking out the machine.'

'You mustn't do that. That machine is of paramount importance.'

'That's how they're getting through, and I'm going to shut it down, one way or another.'

'No.'

'And while you're there, tell the PM to keep the nuclear option open.'

'Don't touch the machine, Thacker. Do you hear me?'

'Try and stop me.' He flicked the phone shut and ignored the immediate call back. 'Radio, now.'

One was pressed into his hands.

'Comms. I want you to get on to Whitehall, find the most senior officer on duty, and tell him I need men, ammunition, tanks, artillery, gunships and ground attack aircraft. With a bit of luck they might offer us a platoon or two.'

There were soldiers, white-faced, running down the

drive. The Warrior had lumbered to life, as had a couple of four-ton trucks and a Land Rover. Their headlights were bright and sharp. They hurt Thacker's eyes and ruined his night vision. He turned away, blinking.

'Move fifty yards out. We'll dig in there and set up a firing line.' As he spoke, he saw thick grey ropes snake out around the front door, feeling its weight before opening it. He shot at the door, and the tentacles rushed back inside. 'Run.'

The four of them ran towards their own advancing line. There were shouts for them to duck, to get out of the way, but Thacker urged those with him on until he thought he'd covered enough ground.

'Down and turn. Fire at will. Aim for the heads.'

And now he could see why the soldiers behind him were so desperate. Ankhani, bloated ichor-filled sacs with glittering eyes, were bounding on their sinuous grey limbs towards him, closing the distance with a tremendous rush of speed. A dozen, two dozen, more, were charging him, spraying black mud in a storm around them.

He was momentarily transfixed, lying on the sodden ground, feeling the moisture wick up beneath him and the rain fall on his back. He heard the man next to him click his rifle to automatic, and the roar of gunfire.

The muzzle flashes were sparks of flame, the empty cases a red-hot cascade of metal that sang over his head. Thacker came to, and tried to pick his targets.

The Ankhani burst and fell, their fragile heads ripped apart by the force of the bullets. As more men lay in the mud and aimed their rifles, the noise grew from singular pops and individual rasps of gunfire into a continuous bellow of rage.

Still they came, pouring through the front doors. The

Warrior trained its cannon there and fired until it ran out of shells.

Thacker retreated from the front line, ordering a dozen men to support those by the kitchen door. Some wise sergeant was issuing fresh clips of ammunition before they were needed.

Two men lifted a fat green crate from one of the trucks.

'Those the missiles?'

'Yes sir.'

'Do you know how to operate them?'

'Yes sir.'

'Get the lid off.'

Thacker picked up an armful and moved to clear ground. The soldier extended the firing tube, flipped up the sights.

'Take out the doors.'

The soldier's colleague checked behind. 'All clear.'

The air shivered, and the missile shrieked towards the Hall, propelled by a shaft of light. It disappeared inside, and a moment later, a flash, a rumble, and the front doors pinwheeled away.

'Next target. First floor, leftmost window.'

The soldier was supplied with a fresh launcher.

'All clear.'

The western edge of the Hall fell on itself. Slates flew from the roof like demented bats.

'Again,' said Thacker.

This time, the outer wall threw itself to the ground in a collapsing sheet of brickwork. Timbers split and floors fell. A blizzard of debris spilled out.

'Good. Now, the banqueting hall.'

The missile there ignited the great pile of wood. Ruddy light began to dance through the windows of Henbury Hall.

The torrent of creatures had slowed to a trickle. Every time one appeared, it was immediately cut down by a hail of bullets to subside in a quivering, pulsating heap.

The fire took hold quickly and hard through the bone dry and desiccated building. It burned so fiercely and thoroughly that Thacker had to pull his troops back twice. Shapes, twisting and writhing, could be seen in the flames.

The gunfire died away, stopping of its own accord. Some men got to their feet, staring into the heat. Others lay their heads down and pressed their cheeks into the slick mud.

Thacker checked. No one had died.

'I suppose,' said Henbury by his ear, 'I should be upset to see it go.'

'How did you get out?'

'I walked. One of the medics leant me these crutches.'

'Someone's going to be on a charge.' Thacker turned back to the blazing house. 'It was almost easy.'

'Only because you had the men and the weapons. Before, there was me and Adams, a pistol and a shotgun. Not so easy, then. If we'd had a regiment and half a dozen gatling guns, I rather think we'd have made a go of it.'

'Yes, I suppose so. My apologies. God, but they're ugly.'

Henbury adjusted his grip on the elbow crutches, his hands still getting used to the plastic handles on the aluminium frame. 'You used rockets. At the machine.'

'I've tried to destroy it. I might even have succeeded. I'm rather assuming they hadn't thought of anti-tank rounds in Pharaoh's day.'

The house growled and shifted. A rush of sparks lifted up into the night sky, winking out one by one.

'Still, it's getting a good roasting,' said Henbury.

'Yes. Tempting to get out the marshmallows, but I shall have to organise my troops, check how much ammunition we have left. If it had gone on much longer, we'd have been down to bayonets.'

'You wouldn't have wanted that.'

'So I understand. We lost one man to those monsters, and that was one too many.' Thacker kicked the ground. 'If it's all the same to you, I'll get someone to escort you back to your tent.'

'Can I keep the crutches?'

'As long as you promise not to go wandering off again.'

'You have my word.'

Thacker walked slowly away, giving orders in a quiet voice as he went. Quite enough excitement for one night, he thought.

Dickson arrived just before dawn. He got Thacker out of bed to survey the damage with him. The embers of Henbury Hall were still glowing red hot, and neither man could approach too closely. Once in a while, something settled in the ruins, releasing a puff of ash and a tongue of fire.

The out-buildings had gone up, too. Their timbers had been baked beyond combustion point by the blaze, and had spontaneously burst into flames.

The air shimmered with heat haze, incongruous on a chill, overcast morning.

'Was it really necessary?'

'Absolutely,' said Thacker, suppressing a vengeful smile. 'There were hundreds of them, and they just kept on coming. For a while, I thought we'd be overwhelmed. One touch from them, and you're dead.'

'So you just mowed them down, then destroyed the house.'

'Not quite how I remember it. I had the house blown up while we were mowing them down, not after. But,' said Thacker, 'you weren't here, and so didn't see how evil they looked. You'd have put a full clip through each one even though one bullet would do. That was our problem in a nutshell. I had to stop them coming out of the hall, and ultimately, the machine, before we had to resort to hand-to-hand combat. If that had happened, you'd be looking at fifty-odd corpses and the countryside swarming with Ankhani.'

'I'm sure I'll read it in your report,' said Dickson, dryly. He tried to peer through the haze. 'That's the west end of the house, over there?'

'You can't see it. It's buried under a section of roof somewhere in that area.'

'Good riddance, you say, I expect.'

'Robert Henbury thought it worthwhile losing his ancestral home for the chance of taking out the machine.'

'Really? Somehow, I couldn't see him moving back in. Thacker, that machine was important, desperately important. They'll want your head on the block for this. You'll get your Court Martial papers by the end of the day, just as soon as the lawyers can work out what charges to bring.'

'And there I was thinking they were going to give me another medal I couldn't tell my family about.'

'I told you the machine had to be saved.'

'The machine was how they got into the hall in the first place. I cut off their retreat and their supply line in one fell swoop. I did go to Sandhurst, you know.'

'You were responsible for saving the machine ...'

'I was responsible for saving the lives of my men and

the civilian population of this county. If this is the way this conversation is going, I'm going to end up punching you and they really will have something to court martial me over.' Thacker turned away for a moment, then back again. 'You didn't see them, coming at us like a flood, like darkness itself was trying to get us. God only knows how the line held, but not one man ran. Not one. You should be proud of them. They did their duty and more, last night.'

'Do you know how much shit I'm going to get over this? We've screwed the Americans around for two days, and we've bugger all to show for it.'

'Dickson, I don't care.'

They stared at each other, waiting for someone to blink. Thacker was damned if he was going to give in, and clearly Dickson felt the same way. Eventually, they were interrupted.

'Mr. Dickson? The fire engines you ordered are here.'

'Right.' He broke away. 'Major Thacker. I think your job here is done. You and your team can head back to Porton Down.'

'As you wish.' Thacker couldn't have been more glad, but it would have been bad form to show it. He turned on his heel and stalked off, every step putting a satisfying distance between him and Dickson.

They'd loaded all their instruments on the back of a truck, and packed up the Warrior with the sensitive papers. Thacker's men were clambering aboard a second truck, when he had a sudden, perverse thought.

Inside the tent, Henbury and Adams were dozing on their cots. They hadn't had much sleep last night, and for the everlasting night before it, trapped in the Hall in some netherworld.

'You've got a choice. You can stay here with Dickson, or you can come with me. It might be that I have to hand you back at some stage, but since possession is nine-tenths of the law, I can make that as easy or as difficult as I like.'

Adams sat up, and looked at Henbury.

'I'm not saying that I'm not going to ask you a thousand and one questions or use you as subjects in medical tests,' continued Thacker, 'but I will ask your permissions first.'

'I don't think we'll get the same from Dickson, sir,' said Adams.

'I think you're right.' Henbury swung his leg out over the edge of the camp bed and Adams levered him upright. 'Won't he try and stop you?' he asked Thacker.

'Only if I, or someone else, tells him. And he's busy trying to retrieve what's left of the machine. He'll need lifting gear. I told him there's part of the roof on top of it.'

'That'll keep the cove occupied. Come on, Adams. Pass me those crutches and we'll throw ourselves on the mercy of the Major.'

With a nod to the guards, Thacker led Henbury and Adams to his waiting Land Rover. 'Get in.'

'Should we lie down?'

'Only if you want to make yourselves really uncomfortable. Trust me, you're part of this convoy and no one wants to inspect the vehicles of a biological weapons unit. They just want to get rid of us as quickly as possible.'

Thacker jumped into the front seat, and tapped the dashboard. The driver started the engine and headed slowly towards the stretch of country road they'd driven in on.

'Don't look so nervous,' said Thacker. 'You're

supposed to be here, yes?'

Both his passengers were sweating, and looking around with sharp, bird-like movements.

They turned onto the road, and started to speed away. Down in the valley, the column of dirty smoke rising into the air was now joined by a twin of steam, as the fire engines damped down the embers.

'Will he find it?' asked Henbury.

'Of course he will. Pieces of it, all over. He might even be able to put it together again, but he'll never make it work.'

'And if he does?'

'We'll shoot the Ankhani, one by one, or by the hundreds, just like we did last night. Time has marched on, gentlemen. We can destroy things now in ways you never dreamed possible.'

# 7

Henbury and Adams thought that the motorway was a dangerous insanity, and anyone who travelled on it had no regard for their own, or anyone else's safety. Despite being limited to fifty by the Warrior, and that both men had travelled far faster on trains, they were amazed and appalled in equal measure by the sheer recklessness of the driving.

'How is all this necessary?' asked Henbury

'Someone decided in the sixties that it would be a good idea. There wasn't half of the traffic volume there is now, and your average car struggled to get to seventy. These days, everyone's a racing driver, and it's all so terribly important to get where you're going quickly.'

'Is it?'

'No.'

They passed the sign which welcomed them to Wiltshire, and Thacker's phone trilled. He checked the dialling-in number, and recognised it as Dickson's.

'I think we've been rumbled,' he said to his passengers, and let the voice-mail take the message.

He gave enough time for a furious Dickson to scorch a set of choice expletives into a digital recorder somewhere in Britain, then retrieved the message with some apprehension.

At first, he couldn't make out what was going on. The sound quality was awful. What he could hear concerned him enough to ask the driver to pull over onto the hard shoulder. The truck and the Warrior pulled in behind the Land Rover, and Thacker pressed his ear hard against the tiny loudspeaker on his handset.

There were screams. Real screams of anguish, of men who wanted to die but couldn't. There was crying, bitter sobbing that came from the pit of the stomach. And there was Dickson whispering over the top of it all: 'Come. Worship. Bow down and worship our new god.'

Thacker felt faint and nauseous. Dickson wasn't one to play a trick, was he? One way to find out. 'I'll be back in a minute.'

'What's the matter, Major? You're as white as a ghost.'

Thacker brushed off Henbury's concern and ran back to the truck where his men were wedged in with the crates of equipment. 'Get on the radio. See if you can raise anyone at Henbury Hall.'

'What's up, sir?'

'I don't know. I think there's been an accident of some sort.'

The radio operator turned on his rig and searched the airwaves. 'There's a carrier, but no traffic.'

Thacker tried his phone. Dickson's mobile was busy. 'Okay, listen. We're going back. We'll stop just outside the first checkpoint, and see what's what.'

He told the same to the Warrior driver, and then to his own.

'Henbury, Adams. I can't let you go. I'm sorry. We have to go back and see what's wrong.'

'What did Dickson say?' asked Adams. 'What aren't you telling us?'

'I'm not sure it was Dickson. Not anymore. I can't raise anyone at the site, either. We've lost contact with them all.'

He dialled the Ministry of Defence, and explained the

problem.

'Just let us out,' said Adams as they drove up the slip road at the next junction. 'Please, Major.'

'I need you, Adams. I need you to tell me what's happening back there.'

'How can we tell you what we don't know?'

'I think you do know. I think if you wrack your brains hard enough you can give me the answers I'm looking for. If I were the Ankhani, and I'd suffered wholesale slaughter, what would I do?'

'You'd run. Lick your wounds. They're cowards, all of them.'

'Of course they are. But don't you think they'd want to take revenge as well?'

'Yes. I don't see …'

'I do,' said Henbury. 'And I've told you already.'

'That's it. You did. You said that Jack thought the Ankhani were going to turn him into a god. I think they have. And they've sent him through from their world to ours. Jack Henbury is our new god.'


The checkpoint was deserted. There should have been a couple of bored coppers who waved away journalists with talk of a chemical spill and the possibility of contamination.

The police car was there, but no police. There were outside broadcast vans, too, parked in a field in neat rows. No sign of life from them, either.

Thacker stopped the convoy, and got everyone out.

'We have another situation, potentially worse than the last one. We all saw what happened last night, when those creatures came at us out of the hall. There was a machine inside, built by Robert Henbury's cousin, Jack, out of parts he found in Egypt. Once activated, that machine opens a gate between two places, two worlds if you like. We stopped the monsters, but something far worse has probably now come through. You'll know him when you see him and you will shoot to kill.

'Now, I'm going on alone. There's no point in risking any more lives than absolutely necessary. I'm reactivating Captain Henbury's commission, which isn't normally the done thing, but this isn't a moment to stick with the book. He'll need a lot of help, but he's an officer, and you'll follow his orders. That all right, Henbury?'

Henbury, on his crutches, swallowed hard and nodded. Thacker handed him his automatic.

'There's a village down the road, Isherwood. Take over the church hall, or the pub if they haven't got one. Evacuate the villagers, at gun point if necessary, and call the Ministry. I hope to God they're taking this seriously. Give me a radio, and I'll keep in touch.'

Thacker strapped the radio to his belt, and commandeered a rifle.

'Right, Henbury, they're all yours. Good luck.'

'And you, Major.' They shook hands awkwardly.

Thacker started to jog down the road to the Hall, keeping next to the hedge to obscure his progress. There was still smoke coming from the valley, a thin reed of soot climbing to the cloud base. The steam of earlier had dispersed.

Round the next corner was the second checkpoint, which should have been manned by soldiers. Thacker crept through the hedge and came up on its blindside.

The concertina of razor wire was still across the road. There was no one else around. The guards had abandoned their post, and there was no sign of any struggle: no bodies, no blood, no shell cases.

Thacker walked on, cautiously, aware that his boots were the only sound he could hear.

He kept on going up to the hedge, peering around it where it was sparse, through the roots where it was not, trying to see into the valley. The land dipped away from the road. He could see the foreslope, but not the site of the Hall unless he started off across country, where large fields made cover infrequent. He'd stick to the road as it was more sheltered, and he could access the camp without being seen from the main drive.

Time to try the radio.

'Captain Henbury, are you there, over?'

Henbury was clearly fumbling with his handset, receiving instruction on how to use it even as he tried to answer Thacker.

'We're in position in the Bricklayer's Arms. Gratifying to see that pubs haven't changed much. Over.'

'I'm on the access road to the camp. The second checkpoint was unmanned as well. So far, so good. I haven't got sight of the house yet. Over.'

'There are units of something called the Army Air Corps on their way. They intend to overfly the area in what? A helicopter? No, it doesn't matter.'

'I'm coming up to the third cordon. I'll speak to you later. Over and out.'

The barricade should have consisted of a Land Rover and two soldiers in NBC suits, guarding a pole slung between two trestles. The men had gone, and on the ground was a respirator. That was it. He looked in the windows of the Land Rover, and in the back, and found it untouched.

'Thacker here,' he said into the radio. 'Checkpoint three is vacant. No clue as to what's happened yet. Over.'

'This is Henbury. This helicopter is going to be with

you in five minutes. They called it an ETA, but I think that's what they meant. Also, we've intercepted a message for Dickson from the British Museum. The machine not only has hieroglyphs on it, but also cuneiform, Sanskrit, something called Linear-A, and Hebrew. They've translated some of the Hebrew, and they say it's a step-by-step guide to assembling the machine itself.'

'What, 'part A goes here' sort of thing?'

'Absolutely. They're going through Jack's notes, but the idiot put sections of it in code. If they uncover anything important, they'll call me direct.'

'Right. I'm going into the camp. Don't call me unless absolutely necessary. I don't want to give my position away. Any last words, Henbury?'

'Don't trust Jack. Whatever happens. Do not trust him an inch.'

'I've every intention of getting rid of him at the earliest opportunity. Over and out.'

Thacker half ran, half scuttled to the gate that led to the camp. Heavy vehicles had churned the ground into a sea of mud, waves of dirt pushed up by fat tyres and dried into place. He crouched down, and checked his rifle. He listened carefully. At the limits of his hearing he could hear the clatter of a low-flying helicopter, drifting in and out as the sound echoed around the valley.

He ran through the mud to the first tent. He burst in, and found nothing but empty camp beds. On a hunch, he rummaged through a couple of the packs and came up with a small pair of binoculars. He slung the cord around his neck, and left the way he had come.

There was no one in the camp. The mess tent still had half-eaten food on the abandoned plates. A big Burco boiler rumbled, full of steam.

Thacker followed the track down to where the main drive started. He hid behind the decontamination tents. The roar of rotor blades was suddenly very loud, and a black shape flashed overhead. The downdraft shook the canvas hard, and Thacker took the opportunity to call Henbury.

'Thacker. In the camp. Still no one. Helicopter is checking. Over and out.'

He watched the helicopter hug the ground into the valley, so low he all but lost sight of it. Then he made a low, crouching run to the first of the dead trees that lined the drive. He crossed the drive, and ducked out of sight again. He could see people now, assembled in a crowd in front of the smouldering pile of rubble that had been Henbury Hall.

He held the binoculars up and tried to work out what they were doing.

There were a mix of people: uniformed soldiers and policemen, white-coveralled technicians, and a good number of civilians. They were all either on their knees or prostrate on the ground in front of a bizarre star-shaped statue.

The helicopter crew clearly couldn't understand it either, because having made one high speed pass, they turned for another go.

Thacker looked again at the statue. On closer inspection, it was vaguely humanoid. Ludicrously long legs splayed, planted on the ground, and arms raised up high. The neck was stretched to impossible lengths, with a tiny head balanced on top, and they were all joined by a torso that struggled to keep the limbs under control.

The statue was moving. The statue was Jack. And the people in front of him were paying him homage, abasing themselves and surrendering their wills to his.

The thought of it made him nauseous. As he scanned the crowd, he saw that every so often, there was a twisted, blackened corpse, still part of the congregation of the damned, but no longer taking any part in the infernal worship.

The helicopter hovered overhead, turning slowly, and Jack turned his baleful gaze upwards. He shifted his stance, ponderously moving one leg, then the other, and he reached up high. The aircraft was out of reach by a good fifty feet, but that didn't seem to matter to Jack.

The fuselage stretched. The tone of the air chopped by the rotors deepened and boomed, and the blades themselves shattered. The helicopter melted in strands of metal and plastic and flesh, dribbling and freezing solid, snapping and clattering to the ground.

In seconds, it was over, and Thacker forced himself to blink. The crowd moaned and cried and wept at the power of this spindly-limbed monstrosity.

'You doubted Me,' said Jack. Not using words, though. The phrase formed complete inside Thacker's head, and made his nose bleed. He choked down his rising gorge.

The people cried and wept more fiercely, desperate. There were shouts of 'No!' and 'Never!'

'Some of you wanted Me to fail.'

There was screaming, and Thacker had to clamp his hand over his mouth to stop himself crying out. The pain was sudden and startling.

Jack reached down and picked up a shrieking man by the neck, as easily as he would pluck a rabbit from a hutch. The man exploded, sending out a shower of blood and offal as an anointing. Jack threw the head aside, and assumed his original star-splayed stance.

'Worship Me.'

Thacker hit his head against the dead trunk of the tree,

once, twice, three times. He now had blood seeping from a gash on his temple and flowing into his eye, but the new pain worked against the old, and freed him from the strange, compelling grip.

He wiped away the blood with his sleeve, tossed the binoculars to one side, and raised his rifle. He leaned over the weapon, sighting carefully, stilling his trembling hands with deep draughts of air.

Where to aim for? The head, of course, but the target was tiny. He'd trained with a rifle, kept all his certificates up to date, but he wasn't the surest shot in the army. The torso, then. The hydrostatic shockwave would be enough to dismember Jack, if he got enough bullets into him.

He settled down, adjusted his sights for range, and selected bursts of three. It was the first time he'd ever attempted deicide.

Jack stepped out of the way of the first shots, moving his body slightly to the right even as Thacker pulled the trigger. The second three were stopped in the flat of Jack's outstretched hand.

Thacker switched to fully automatic, and let the god have it all. He missed with every last bullet, or at least, did not hit with a single one.

Then Jack was striding towards him, and he turned tail and ran. The pressure in his skull was threatening to burst his brains.

'Worm. You dare strike me?'

Stumbling along with his hands pressed to the sides of his head, Thacker gasped. 'I'll dare a bloody sight more, you freak.'

'Blasphemer. Die.'

'Not today.' He gained the camp, and tripped through the forest of guys and pegs.

Jack was slow, as uncertain of his steps as a new-born

deer. Whilst each pace took him twenty feet, he had to steady himself before taking the next. Thacker ran as if the hounds of hell were at his back. But the god's terrified worshipers were driven by more than naked fear. They charged after Thacker, hoping to bring him down, present him as a sacrifice, and gain a moment's rest from a life that now promised nothing but torment.

Many of them were fitter than Thacker, younger than Thacker, plain faster than Thacker. The only thing in his favour was that he had a head start.

He made it into the front seat of an armoured Land Rover, reached across and locked the passenger door, then his own. Jack Henbury loomed large, and his minions flocked around his ankles, desperate to show their devotion and not be left behind.

Thacker prayed for the first time in a long time, and the Land Rover started. He threw it into first and hurtled up the slope to the hedge. He kept waiting for Jack to stop him, to conjure a wall for him to drive into, or melt the vehicle like he'd melted the helicopter and its crew. He could see him in his rear view mirrors.

He was through the hedge. The engine nearly stalled, and Thacker fought to save it, stamping on the clutch and gunning the accelerator. The front wheels bounced across the roadside ditch and hit tarmac. He threw the Land Rover around, tyres screeching, then worked his way through the gears until he was doing a flat out fifty-five.

Jack receded from view.

Thacker roared past the third checkpoint, and didn't even slow for the second, snapping the wooden pole across the road cleanly in two. The first, he had to brake for. Unlocking his door, he brushed the razor wire aside, and didn't bother shutting the door on his way back in.

A signpost for Isherwood flashed by, and Thacker took

the turning, just.

He still had the radio on his belt. One hand on the wheel, he called Henbury.

'Thacker. Lost the helicopter. Crew dead. Barely made it out myself.'

'It's Henbury. Where are you?'

'On the road to Isherwood. I've got Jack and about a hundred, hundred and fifty crazed fanatics chasing me.'

'It is Jack then?'

'I have to assume so. He's now thirty feet tall and can kill by thought alone.' Blood was starting to obscure his vision, but he didn't have a free hand to wipe it away. 'Excuse me a moment.'

He put the radio down on the seat next to him and used an oily rag from the dashboard to mop himself up with.

'Thacker again. I shot Jack repeatedly. He either anticipated where the bullets were going, or caught them in his bare hand. But there's a limit to his powers. I got away by running very quickly, so I'm guessing his influence doesn't extend so far.'

'The Air Corps are here. With more helicopters.'

'Tell them to stand off and fire as soon as they acquire their target. Too close, and they're toast.'

'How close is too close?'

'Good question. Look, it's difficult to drive this thing and talk at the same time. I'll be with you in a couple of minutes. Over and out.'

He could make out a church spire and some red tiled roofs a few fields away. His vision was starting to swim, and he had to shake his head to get rid of the disturbance. Rather than crash at breakneck speed in a narrow country lane, he started to bite his lip, hard.

# 8

Thacker spotted the glint of glass from the church belltower: a spotter with binoculars. He'd been clocked already by the dozen soldiers crouched behind garden walls as he came into the village, and assumed that Henbury had given the order not to fire. A rash decision, but Thacker was grateful.

The village green, more used to maypoles and Morris dancing, looked like an aerodrome from the Vietnam era. There were olive green helicopters as far as he could see, and men running around underneath them, pulling safety pins from red-tipped missiles.

The pub was opposite the green. He braked hard, his senses coming and going: one moment razor-sharp, the next, dreamlike. The wheels skidded, but he held it straight and the Land Rover stopped in a cloud of dust and smoke.

Adams was at the door, opening it, manhandling Thacker out.

'You're buggered up good and proper, Major.'

Thacker grunted. 'How long have we got?'

'Nothing spotted yet.'

'They were right behind me.' He turned around and looked. Just Oxfordshire.

Adams carried him into the pub, and dumped him in a chair opposite Henbury.

'Dear God. Fetch the man a whisky.'

'Actually, I'd prefer a cup of tea.'

'Oh shut up, Major.' A large tumbler brimming with golden liquid was banged onto the table.

Thacker knocked half of it back in one sour-faced gulp. He almost threw up, swallowed hard, and felt the alcohol flood his system like a cold rush.

'That's better.'

'You look a mess.'

'That's what happens when you try to beat your own brains out with a very large tree. Not recommended, but the situation was extreme.' Thacker focussed on the tabletop, where there was a map with arrows drawn on it. 'What's the plan?'

'We have a battalion of these helicopters parked out on the rec, armed with air-to-ground missiles and machine guns. I also have a detachment of maintenance crew in full combat readiness deployed in an arc facing west on the outskirts of the village.'

'The MoD are taking us seriously then?'

'Oh yes, although in my day it was the War Office. Apparently our Mr Dickson has been very busy with his little telephone, calling all sorts of important people and telling them to welcome Jack. We have a column of tanks and artillery coming out from Salisbury, and Guards regiments from London. The Gurkhas are in Hampshire and will probably be the first to reach us.' Henbury took delivery of a foaming pint of bitter and took a long pull. 'In an hour and a half.'

'They expect us to hold the fort till then?'

'I rather think they do. I have, however, called the Chief Constable of Oxfordshire, and he can get us about a hundred armed officers within the hour, and some are already here. Now, what are we facing?'

Thacker sipped some more whisky. It burned his lip where he had bitten it. 'Jack, of course. He has, I suppose, some limited control over things around him. He melted the helicopter as it hovered over him. Melted the crew, too. He blew some unfortunate up as an example to his worshipers. I shot at him, but the bullets never connected. I don't know what to suggest there.'

'Hit him from more than one angle at once? Perhaps he has to be concentrating.'

'It's all guesses, I'm afraid. Then we have his entourage. They might have been our friends, our colleagues, but they'll rip us apart with their bare hands if they get hold of us. Anything for Jack. I'm not looking forward to ordering men to open fire at people they've been drunk with.'

'But if they don't shoot them, they'll die themselves.'

'That's about it.'

'What a bloody awful mess. Damn Jack.'

Thacker raised his glass. 'I'll drink to that.'

Henbury touched his pint mug to the side of Thacker's tumbler. 'What do you think? Is this going to work?'

'That,' said Thacker, 'is in the lap of other gods, who are hopefully more merciful than the one we have out there on the rampage.'

They drank in silence, then Henbury's radio crackled into life.

He picked it up, listened to the message, then put it down, looking thoughtful. 'The observer has reported seeing a strange stilt-man, about three miles away. Jack?'

'Why don't we get those helicopters in the air? I'd like to see if we can take him down before he gets into the village.'

'Rather.' Henbury called to Adams, loitering by the bar. 'Get those whirly things up. Jack's been spotted, five thousand yards west-south-west on the approach road. Tell them to hit him simultaneously. Don't spare the ammunition; this could be the best chance we have.'

Adams trotted out, and Henbury regarded Thacker. 'You ought to let someone take a look at your head. You're bleeding on my map.'

'Sorry.' Thacker tried to wipe the drops of red away, and only succeeded in smearing it across Home Farm and Foundry Brook.

Henbury gathered his crutches and eased himself out of his seat. 'You coming to watch?'

Thacker nodded, and paused only to pick up a beer-soaked bar towel. He held it to his head as he stood next to Henbury in the porch.

Starter motors whined, then engines roared. Rotor blades started taking fat bites out of the air, and the sound blended into one almighty roar. The first helicopter rose, leant forward, and started to climb. One after another, eight in all, they took off, circled, then formed up in a line facing west.

Adams emerged out of the shivering haze of dust. 'Funny to think. Those strange machines stand between us and the end of England.'

The helicopters moved off, low, just clearing the tree line.

'Right,' said Henbury. 'Let's try and co-ordinate this attack.'

They had barely sat down around the map when the rocket salvo started. They leaned forward, bending their ears to the squawk of the radio. It took little more than two minutes for the helicopters to fire all their missiles. Thacker imagined how it would look:

great dirty fireballs hurling themselves into the summer sky, earth and stone thrown high into the air, men and women cowering around the stick-thin legs of Jack Henbury as they pleaded with him to save them. Dickson, perhaps, too. Proud Dickson, guardian of national security now praying to his new god to destroy the attackers that used to be under his command.

Jack, of course, caring nothing for the worthless lives that teemed around his feet, bleating like sheep who had fallen in with wolves. There were always more humans to fall on their faces in front of him, billions more.

But now the men in their flying machines resisted him like that soldier had done earlier when he had tried to shoot him. This new enemy used bigger weapons, and it was difficult to control their paths, to change the warp and weft of space/time. It could be done, though; as long as he let his followers take their own chances.

The captain in charge of the flight reported back to Henbury: 'No effect. Repeat. No effect.'

'Disengage now, Captain. Get away as far and fast as you can. Spotter, what can you see?'

'One helicopter is in trouble, sir. The others seem to be breaking off. On the ground, there's some movement. Five, maybe six people.'

'What of Jack?'

'The stilt-man has stopped. Now he's turning away. Heading north.'

'Blast him, where's he off to?' Henbury looked at the map, then at the tiny legend at its very edge. 'Banbury, six miles. How big is Banbury now?'

Thacker threw the bar towel to the floor, where it

smacked wetly on to the stone flags. 'A damn sight bigger than it was eighty years ago. Henbury, I want you to get everyone together and follow him. Shoot at him all the way. Slow him down. Buy some time.'

'And what are you going to do?'

'I'm going back to the Hall. I'm going to turn that machine off, one way or another. Adams, I want you to come with me.'

'Me? Why?'

'I want someone who's not afraid of Ankhani. And someone who can drive.'

Adams looked at Henbury, who nodded slowly.

'Right then.' He saluted stiffly. 'Good luck, sir.'

'You too, Adams. Look after the major.' Henbury turned his attention to the radio, and Thacker stumbled out into the daylight.

The air was thick with the smell of spent explosives and burnt flesh. Adams must have smelled it in the trenches a hundred times before, but it was new to Thacker. It made his gorge rise, and he struggled to control it.

His head was still bleeding. Henbury had been right when he'd suggested a medic. There was always too little time to do a proper job on anything.

'Adams. In the back of that lorry you'll find two crates of grenades. Get them in the back of the Land Rover while I make a call.' He took out his mobile and sat on one of the rustic benches in front of the pub.

The man on duty at the MoD knew his name, and Thacker surmised he had gone up in the world somewhat since the morning, when Dickson had threatened him with Court Martial.

He found himself talking to the Minister of State himself.

'Sir, I wanted to know if a decision had been made regarding a nuclear strike.'

Thacker eased himself into the passenger seat, and found Adams trying to familiarise himself with the controls of the Land Rover.

'Don't worry. This heap is nearly as old as I am. All the gears have synchromesh, so just depress the clutch, wrestle it into first, and stamp on the accelerator.'

Adams didn't make a move. 'That phone call you made. Will it hurt Master Robert?'

'I won't lie to you, Adams,' said Thacker. 'I'm trying my very utmost to persuade someone to drop a bloody big bomb on Jack before it's too late.'

'How big?'

'It'll leave a crater half a mile wide and incinerate most of Banbury if it gets in the way.'

'You can do that?'

'And even then I don't know if it'll stop him. But I think we're going to have to try.' He pushed away the line of blood drawing down his face. 'It might help if we can get the machine out of commission. He could be using it as some sort of power source. Close it down, weaken him to a point where conventional weapons would work. To answer your question, Robert Henbury and everyone else sniping at Jack's heels will vanish in a puff of light.'

Adams put his hand on the gear stick and ground it into position. The Land Rover lurched, executed a tight U-turn and headed back down the road towards the hall.

After a while, he spoke. 'I lived my life for that man. There's nothing odd about it, so don't snigger. I'd die for him. Nearly have done, several times. I can't let him die now, after everything we've gone through. The war. The house. Now this. Tell me honestly: where am I better off serving him? Here with you, or with him?'

'Slow down for the craters,' said Thacker. The tarmac was deeply pitted where the missiles had fallen. There were bodies, too, and parts of bodies. The ruined remains of what had been once a helicopter lay upside down in a field of young wheat. He let Adams navigate the obstacles before replying.

'I don't know for sure. I'm guessing, your coming with me.'

'That'll do for now, I suppose.'

'I've seen men crack before, men who'd look down their noses at you, Adams, because you're a rough spoken, ill-educated gardener. I think you're a bloody marvel. You've been thrown in at the deep end; didn't ask for any of this, did you?'

'Can't say I did, Major.' The Land Rover lurched as it came over the lip of the final crack in the road. Adams put his foot down, and eventually selected a higher gear.

'I hope, when all this is done, you can find yourself some sort of life here. I'll do my damndest to make sure that happens. I mean,' said Thacker, 'Government ministers take my telephone calls. That has to count for something.'

'You can hope so.' Adams was gripping the steering wheel tight as he negotiated one tight turn after another.

Then, just after they swept past the first abandoned checkpoint, they came across an Ankhani, walking down the road toward them.

'Damn!' yelled Adams, trying to find the brakes.

They hit it square on, the bonnet taking its tentacles out from underneath it. The bloated body smacked against the windscreen and burst, black liquid spraying out like thrown paint. The windscreen itself starred and bowed inwards, frost forming on it, but the glass just held.

The Land Rover squealed to a halt, and Thacker grabbed his rifle before getting out to inspect the damage.

There was smoke coming from the engine. When Thacker looked closer, the bonnet itself had split, and ichor was leaking in. The impact had dented the bumper by far more than he would have expected.

'For something with no bones, they seem pretty solid.'

Adams opened his door and leaned out. 'Behind you.'

Thacker crouched and turned. Two more Ankhani emerged from around the next corner. They saw him at the same time as he saw them. He shot at them, and missed. They ducked back out of sight.

'The place is crawling with them. We have to get to the machine.' Thacker jumped back in. 'Can you see around that mess?'

'Mostly,' said Adams. 'I take it I don't stop until we get there.'

'I think you've got it. Try not to run any more of them over, no matter how tempting. One more hit like that, and we're walking.'

Adams drove on, slowly and steadily. There was no sign of the Ankhani save for frost-blackened gaps in the hedge. 'Shouldn't you report this?'

'Yes, but I'm not going to. I want those in charge to concentrate on Jack, not get distracted by a few monsters. When they've dealt with him, we can mop up the rest. Listen, Adams: do the Ankhani see us as a threat? Are they scared of us?'

Adams, dodging his head around the broken part of the windscreen and spilt ichor, took a moment to answer.

'They seemed wary. But they didn't seem to be scared of death. I think if there was a chance of a meal, they'd have a go. Getting shot was just one of those things, like they'd just lost a few farthings at cards.'

Thacker rubbed his chin, found more blood on it, and traced the sticky trail upwards to his head. He wiped as much as he could away with his sleeve. 'I was hoping for a more human reaction: asking too much, I suppose.'

They passed the second checkpoint. There were more burnt holes in the hedgerows. Thacker began to feel uneasy. Adams voiced his own concern.

'Just how many of the buggers are there?'

'When you went through for Jack, how many did you see?'

'Hardly any. A dozen, two dozen maybe.'

'We killed hundreds last night. I wonder if I've done the right thing.'

The final checkpoint was just before the main drive. Three Ankhani were clustered around the body of a small deer. They were breaking brittle pieces off, holding them for a moment, then throwing them away. As they heard the engine rev, they turned sharply, then ran off in three different directions.

'What's the plan?' asked Adams.

'Drive to the machine, as close as we can. Put the boxes of grenades next to it, and blow them all up.' Thacker checked his rifle, then Adams' gun. 'Not much of a plan, but if it doesn't work, we'll have to think of something more imaginative.'

Adams turned into the driveway.

There were Ankhani as far as the eye could see.

Thacker gaped.

'They've spotted us. What do I do?' said Adams.

'There must be thousands of them.'

'What do you want me to do?'

'I …'

'Major? Oh damn it all to hell.' Adams started forward,

picking up speed, working his way through the gears.

The Land Rover shuddered with each blow. Some were glancing, merely throwing the vehicle off to one side and causing Adams to wrestle with the steering wheel like he was in the teeth of an Atlantic gale. Others were head on, and it was like charging concrete bollards. The windscreen froze over, cracked and cracked again until it was a single web of white lines that was impossible to see through. The side windows were streaked with frost and smears of black blood that blocked out the light just as thoroughly.

'I don't know where I'm going,' shouted Adams.

'Keep it straight.' Thacker banged out a section of windscreen with his rifle butt. He saw the remains of the hall dead ahead, before he had to duck. A spray of liquid splattered his seat, and he sat up again. 'Almost there.'

There was a massive lurch to the right, and another to the left as Adams tried to compensate. Thacker was thrown forward, then back.

'Lost a wheel.'

They were slowing, slowing.

'Another ten yards, Adams.'

The speedometer read less than twenty. Thacker thought that it was over, that it had all been in vain, when suddenly they were airborne. The engine raced, and the front of the Land Rover tipped down.

They hit hard. The windscreen finally gave in a cascade of fragments. Thacker and Adams hit their spines going down against cab coming up. The dashboard was a blaze of red lights.

There were the briefest moments of peace, as they surveyed the ruins of Henbury Hall from an intimate vantage point. A cloud of ash and brick dust started to settle around them.

Something scuttled across the top of the vehicle.

Thacker brought his rifle up and sent three rounds past his own ear.

Adams was wrestling with his door catch. The mechanism had jammed.

'Out through the front. I'll cover you.'

Adams threw his gun out, then himself on to the shattered bonnet while Thacker raked the roof of the Land Rover. Hot metal flew everywhere, hurting him. The noise was deafening, the situation desperate.

'Come on, man!' shouted Adams. 'Now!' He put the butt of his rifle to his shoulder and fired single shots, miserly with his ammunition.

Thacker heaved himself out, rolled off into the still-warm ash and blackened timbers. 'Where's the machine?'

'We landed square on it.'

Thacker finally realised that they'd driven through the stump of the front wall and fallen through to the cellar. Dickson had managed to remove enough of the debris to expose the machine, and now the wreck of their transport lay directly on top of it.

The Ankhani had gathered around the rim of the cellar. There were far too many to kill.

He looked for another way out, and saw it in the strange, vision-warping pool of darkness that hovered above the rubble. The machine was on its side. So was the door to the Ankhani's world.

'Adams? They're going to rush us any second.'

'What are we going to do?'

Thacker reached out and grabbed Adams by his arm. He was all skin and bones, and he let Thacker spin him around so that he was between him and the door.

Thacker jumped, pushing Adams in front of him. They fell.

# 9

One moment he was falling down, then falling sideways. He was totally unprepared for the abrupt twist in vertical and landed face first in the grey dust of the Ankhani's world.

Up close, it was the same fine, desiccated debris that lay around the hall. Long, long ago, those cold, greedy creatures had used up all the vital energy of their once life-giving planet. Now they used their science to suck it from other, younger realms.

Adams was on his feet quickly, turning and looking for a target. 'I swore I'd die rather than come back here, Major.'

'And we would have died.' Thacker spat out grey phlegm and picked up his own appallingly dusty rifle.

'There's nothing for us here. If they shut the door on us, we're trapped forever. The last bullet will be for me, but the second to last is yours if you don't think of something fast.'

'Get a grip, man. The Land Rover is on top of the machine. They can't get to the controls.' He looked back at the floating door, the hole in the air that led back to the hall. At first he could see only sky, but by looking obliquely through it, he caught glimpses of fallen wall, broken vehicle, shifting ash.

'But we can't go back.'

'There must be something here.'

'No Ankhani. They've all crossed over.'

The landscape was barren. Devoid of anything, living or dead, and ground down through aeons of wear that the highest relief was a small hill. Perhaps once it had been a mountain to rival Everest: now it was only a pimple on a plain.

Adams looked around for a second time. 'We need to get to the Cathedral.'

'The what?'

'The place where they took Jack for his … changing. It's a sort of building.'

'Where is it?'

'If we climb the hill, we can see it.'

The Ankhani sky was populated by dim, blood red suns, exhausted to the point of collapse. Thacker nodded. 'Be lucky to see anything in this light.'

'You get used to it.'

'I'm sorry, Adams. I thought what I did was best. I wasn't going to let those monsters take us.'

Adams kicked the ground. 'I meant what I said, although I suppose we can have a look, see what we can find.'

'Thank you.'

Thacker had been an army officer for a long time, long enough for most of the people he knew to be in the army or connected with it in some way. People who were used to either giving orders or being ordered. Adams was neither to him, and it was Adams who had realised it first.

So they walked side by side up the hill, and from the top they could see in the distance a tall spire that seemed to grow straight from the blighted ground.

'I take it that's it.'

'There were Ankhani there, in the shadows. They didn't interfere with us, mind. Just looked on.' Adams' expression showed he'd rather go anywhere than that grotesque building. 'I don't know why. They could have killed us a hundred times over.'

'Second guessing these things is pointless. They do what they do because they want to.' Thacker gazed at the spire. 'Or they have to: biological imperative and all that.'

They kicked dust as they walked, Thacker's stride becoming increasingly weary.

'When we were here before, Master Robert thought we might be a very long way from home. He couldn't recognise any of the stars in the sky. Have your astronomers found their planet?'

'They're your astronomers, too, Adams. No, I don't think so. I don't even know if this place should exist. The sky back home is full of bright stars, wherever you look, however far away you look. Here, it's dead. Like we're at the very end of time itself.' Thacker looked up again at the dying light. 'Einstein said space and time were the same thing, that one was just an expression of the other. I suppose, there might be some part of the universe like this – the first to be created would be the first to dissolve back into the void.'

'Some Eden,' snorted Adams.

'Perhaps they fell further than your name-sake.'

They had arrived at the cathedral. It was fantastically tall, stretched like Jack Henbury to be a hideous parody of what it faintly resembled. Walls flowed like molten skin, arches stretched like strands of mucus, the dark spaces breathed in restless sleep.

'We went in,' said Adams, seeing Thacker hesitate.

'You're a braver man than me.'

'That might be so, but it's a long way to come for nothing.' He stepped over the threshold, and let his eyes accustom to the gloom.

Thacker held his rifle ready, and reluctantly joined

him.

Inside, it only had the semblance of darkness. Thacker found that he could see rather well. The walls themselves seemed to ooze weak light like a cave sweats beads of moisture. There were no shadows: only his and Adams' bodies were formless because they were unlit.

In the first large hall, they found Jack's instrument of torture, a great shining metal wall streaked with blood and excrement, tears and sweat.

As Thacker looked up at it, Adams spoke quietly in his ear. 'Would you do it? Would you give yourself up to pain like you never knew before, just to save England?'

'If it was the only way? I don't know. But we haven't got eighty years. We need something that'll work now.' And Thacker was glad that he didn't have to step up to the wall and let it tear him apart as it turned him into a god.

Adams went to look in another aisle, and came back shortly to report: 'You'd better take a look at this.'

What he found was the junkyard of millennia. Everything the Ankhani had ever used and exhausted, they seemed to have thrown away here. It stretched, a pile of jumble tossed against one long wall, forever. Most of it had turned to dust, but there were objects embedded in that dust, shapes of promise and warning like bones in a grave.

Thacker chose at random, and dipped his hand in. He came out with a deeply corroded metal bar, as thick as his finger in some places, and pitted to within a hair's breadth of snapping in others.

'This is hopeless,' he said. 'We could search from now until Doomsday and not cover a tenth of this.' He threw the bar back, and watched as it fell into the dust and was instantly lost.

'Then we look somewhere else,' said the ever-practical Adams. 'Somewhere we can see what we're looking at.'

'But what if it's here? The very thing we're looking for?'

'You'll have to pray it's not.'

'Damn you, Adams!'

'Damn you too. I never wanted to come here. I would rather have taken my chances with the monsters and had an end to it all.'

Thacker put his hand to his head. It was still bleeding, and he wondered how much blood he'd lost. He felt awful; tired beyond belief, unable to string two thoughts together without the utmost concentration, and above all, weak. 'We have to try, man. It's what makes us who we are.'

'Then get up, Major. Get up and try.'

Thacker realised he'd slumped to his knees. He used the rifle to lever himself upright, and staggered off like a drunkard.

They walked through the vast spaces of the cathedral, looking at the heaps of aeons-old debris, scattering some, leaving others, despairing always.

Then at the moment they thought it useless, they came to an armoury.

At first, they didn't know what it was: a space, like all the others, different but the same, but this time with massive stone sarcophagi on the ground. The tapered boxes were thick with dust, time having smoothed the edges and erased any symbols.

'These are huge,' said Thacker, putting down his rifle and running his hands over the lid of the first one.

'Shaped like coffins,' said Adams. 'Are you sure you want to open one?'

'No. But this is the only thing we've found that hasn't crumbled to dust.' He put his shoulder to it, and made no impression.

Adams joined him, and they strained together. The lid moved a fraction.

'Again,' said Thacker, 'we have to push harder.'

It moved again, enough to get the rifle butt in and use it as a lever. Thacker hardly dared look at the contents before the lid was off completely, but he caught glimpses of dull metal in familiar shapes below.

The lid teetered and slipped. It fell with a huge concussion, and split in two ragged halves.

They waited for the cloud of disturbed dust to die down, and looked over the rim.

'In those days,' quoted Thacker, 'giants dwelt in the land.'

Inside the sarcophagus was a suit of armour that Goliath might have worn. Bigger than that, even: Thacker could barely lift the sculpted helmet from the tomb.

'If you thought you could wear that and fight Jack, you're wrong.' Adams picked up a spear resting by the suit, and almost toppled backwards.

Thacker put the helmet down on one of the other boxes and inspected it. It had a visor he could move, on which was carved a stylised face – noble, straight nose, high and sharp cheeks, a mouth curved like a bow and framed with a curled beard. Yet the space inside was small. His head would be a snug fit.

He reached back down for one of the segmented gauntlets. Again, the outside was huge, a giants' hand. Inside, he would barely able to wriggle his fingers.

'Get everything out,' he said. 'I think I know what this is.'

Adams sighed, and started emptying the sarcophagus. 'You have to be joking. This breastplate is as big as a table.'

'Remember the myths and fables? Where a mere man fights dragons and Cyclops and half-men, half-beasts? The heroes of old? Hector, Achilles, Ajax, Jason? Gilgamesh, even. This isn't a suit of armour for a giant. This is a suit of armour for a hero.'

'That bang on your head has sent you crazy.'

'Help me put it on.'

'It's a trap. Everything these monsters ever made was a trap. Like the machine. Just like the machine.'

'I'm sorry, Adams. I have to see what happens, and I'd rather it was me than you.'

'No. You'll turn into something terrible.' Adams brought up his gun. 'You can't do that to me.'

Thacker stood still. 'Do we have a choice?'

Adams swallowed hard. Eventually, the barrel of his gun wavered, then dipped. 'All those heroes came to a sticky end. They did things that weren't right, even though they started out good. They ended up bad.'

'It just has to hold together long enough for me to take on Jack. That's all. I've no dreams of divinity.'

Adams dropped his rifle. 'Then I won't be needing that anymore. When we've done you, and if it works as you think, then getting another lid off shouldn't be a problem at all.'


He started at the feet, kicking off his own army boots and pulling on the heavy footwear from the base of the sarcophagus. They made him look ridiculous, great outsized things like he was off for a fortnight's skiing. He could barely lift his legs in them.

'This is all wrong. It's not going to work.'

'Shut up and stand still. A few moments of feeling daft won't hurt.' Adams offered up a piece of leg armour to

Thacker's shin and it almost fitted itself, tripping catches that locked it onto the top of the boot. 'See?'

Slowly, British Army khaki gave way to dull Persian bronze. He was encased in metal: arms, legs, chest; each segment slipping into place and holding itself fast.

Finally, the helmet, which would add almost another foot to his height.

'Do you feel any different?' asked Adams.

'I feel wretched. We've wasted all this time, and Jack's still moving towards Banbury. He could be there by now.'

Adams stood on tiptoe and let the helmet slide down onto the neck ring. It clicked.

'How about now?' he said.

Thacker was scared to move. If he fell over, Adams wouldn't have the strength to lift him up, and would have to spend the next few hours working out how to get him out again.

He took a tentative step, no more than a shuffle. He jumped like his feet had springs. He hit a wall, and on trying to recover, span and reached out for the edge of the stone sarcophagus. It shattered in his grasping hands.

Adams was cowering in a corner. 'Stop, Major, stop!'

Thacker gained control of the armour that seemed to amplify and exaggerate every move he made. Carefully, he picked up the sarcophagus lid that it had taken the two of them to painfully lever off, and threw it. It sailed through the air and crashed onto the floor, snapping in two uneven pieces with the force of the impact.

'That does it,' he said. His voice was distorted in his ears, shouted out through the mouthpiece of the visor loud enough to make the chamber ring.

Adams got to his feet and approached in awe. 'Bugger me,' he said, 'It does work.'

'I have to go and fight Jack. Now.'

'But what about me? We'll need both of us.'

'The army will shoot me on sight, and you too, if you're in this get-up. I need you as you are, to vouch for me.'

'You said …'

'I didn't. You assumed, and I didn't tell you otherwise. You've gone through too much, Adams, you've fought your battle and you've survived. I'm not asking you to do any more than to get me to Jack.'

'But I want to!'

'I know. But I won't let you, and now, you can't stop me. I'm going back, and I'm assuming that you don't want to stay here.' Thacker reached out and, as gently as he could, lifted Adams up off the ground with one hand. The metal armour creaked softly. With his other hand he picked up the spear and the shield that was as big as the Round Table.

He put Adams on his shoulder, where the man clung like a child, and then he started to run like he had never run before. He passed in two steps through rooms that previously had seemed endless; moving so fast that everything was a blur. Adams' thin scream trailed out behind them like a wisp of smoke.

Out, out of the cathedral, running like his feet were on fire, up to the hill then a change in direction to head for the tiny circle of tantalising blue sky in the distance.

At some point, Adams managed to draw breath. He hit Thacker on the helmet with the flat of his hand in an attempt to attract his attention. Thacker became aware of the annoyance and slowed to a halt just before the door.

'What? What is it?'

'It's starting already, Major. You're forgetting who you are. And you're not like Jack. You can be hurt in this armour. Before you go through, you need a plan: a good plan, mind.'

The hero's suit of armour seemed to accelerate everything except his mind. Adams was right. He had to think first. He had to assume that he wasn't indestructible.

'The Land Rover is still on the machine, and the back of it is still full of grenades. I'll set fire to the fuel tank, and that should give us enough time to get away. Then on to Jack.'

'What about the Ankhani?'

'I don't know. I should be able to hold them off with these.' He brandished his weapons.

'I was thinking more about me. There are a lot of them. One touch, remember.'

Think, Thacker, think. 'Climb on my back. Hold on. It's the best I can do.'

'The old Major would have cared more.' Adams clambered up and stretched his arms around Thacker's massive neck. He could just about grip his own wrists, but there was little purchase lower down. The metal was too slick, and his feet slid off.

'You can't do it.' Thacker was impatient, and he caught himself resenting Adams. 'You'll have to get further up.'

When Adams was sitting astride the armour's shoulders and clinging to the stylised crown on top of the carved helmet, he was satisfied.

'Ready?'

'Don't turn your head quickly, Major. I'll fall.'

Thacker ignored the man's warning. He shifted the spear to his right hand and put his left forearm through the straps on the shield. The lion design on the face of it saw the light of day for the first time in four thousand years as it led the way back to Henbury Hall.

# 10

The contrast in light was abrupt. Before, everything was dark and dismal. Now it was bright and sharp like lightning. Thacker leaped from the door of the machine, orientated himself to the shift in gravity, and strode out into a sea of shifting rubble, swinging his spear in short, predatory arcs.

The Ankhani reacted, as far as he could tell, firstly with astonishment, then fear. They stopped their probing of the wrecked Land Rover, and as he turned to face them, they started backing away.

Thacker wondered if the armour was Ankhani-made after all, whether it was originally of human artifice, whether it had been designed to combat gods and monsters from the dawn of time, whether the Ankhani had taken the hero suits back to their own world and hidden them away so that they no longer presented a threat to their power.

The creatures would run into a blizzard of machine gun fire, but shrank from a man in brazen armour, wielding a spear and shield. He had to make the most of it, while he had the advantage.

With Adams still clinging to him, he leapt forward and plunged the spear deep into the heart of the Land Rover's engine. Metal on metal shrieked and sparked. He twisted the leaf-shaped blade this way and that, scraping the point across the ruined engine block.

'That's not going to do it,' shouted Adams. He let go

his death-grip on Thacker's head and dropped to the floor. He scrambled into the cab and reached through to the crates of grenades. He grabbed one at random, and struggled back out.

Thacker jumped up to the ruined ground floor and darted at the mass of Ankhani. They flowed before him like a great dark tide, deciding not to get close to him even though their numbers were such that they could have overwhelmed him in seconds.

It felt to Thacker like he was in control, actually master of his own destiny for the first time in days.

'Major! Remember Jack.'

How he would have liked to have chased the Ankhani, spearing them one after another until the ground ran black with ichor. But Adams had called him to his senses. With a final defiant flourish of his shield, he dropped back down to the cellar.

'Can you throw this accurately?' Adams presented him with a phosphorous grenade.

'Of course.'

'I need to be well away when it goes off. You'll need to protect me, even if you can stand the blast.' Again, Adams had to remind Thacker of his frailty.

'Yes, yes.' He crouched down and Adams climbed up to his perch. Barely before he'd settled, Thacker was off, running to the far edge of the ruins.

When he judged the distance safe, he took the grenade, pulled the pin, and threw it in a low, tight arc. The bomb slotted into the space where the windscreen used to be, and suddenly white fire boiled out.

Adams slipped off and pressed himself behind two courses of brick. Thacker stood and watched as the Land Rover burned brightly enough to cast a shadow. With a shattering crack, and a blast of heat straight from the furnaces of hell, the grenades exploded.

A churning ball of flame flashed out and up, the air stiffened, the ground trembled. He watched it all. He looked into the heart of the inferno and stared it down. The fireball mounted a dirty pillar of dust and smoke, and roiled into the sky.

Eventually, he blinked, looked down, and saw that the machine was ripped apart. There were shards of it everywhere, scattered around him like bright tears.

'You can get up now,' he said to Adams.

'Is it gone?'

'Destroyed. Forever.'

The Ankhani were fleeing, scattering in the Oxfordshire countryside, slipping through hedgerows and leaving only frost-marks in their wakes.

'They'll kill plenty before they're all caught,' said Adams.

'They're nothing. Forget them.' Thacker turned his gaze to the east and the west, then finally to the north. 'That way. I can feel him like a pain in my head.'

'Major? Go back to the camp first.'

'That's wasting time.'

'You want me to get you to Jack? Go to the camp.'

Thacker picked Adams up roughly and carried him over the rubble and up the driveway to the camp.

'Damn you, man, you'll break me,' Adams snarled at Thacker, who didn't care. After looking to his new bruises, he took the Union flag that had been draped over the guys of a tent and told Thacker to tie it to his spear. 'With that, the Army might just hesitate long enough to listen to an explanation.'

He disappeared into another tent, and emerged with some spare fatigues. He changed out of his white coverall and into khaki.

'Now, Adams. Now.' Thacker had run out of patience.

Adams tied the last shoelace. 'Done. Now run like you've the very devil at your back.'


They went straight across country, as the crow would fly and the fox would hunt. Thacker found that he could hurdle hedgerows almost without breaking step. Landing from such a height didn't affect him at all, but poor Adams suffered grievously from the shocks and knocks that he carelessly received.

In copses of trees, Thacker would dart athletically between the trunks, leaving his passenger to be lashed by the overhanging branches. He would leap streams and gullies and almost shake Adams off with the impact.

On and on, always northward, guided by some enhanced sense of Thacker's until they could hear the rattle of small arms fire and the crunch of mortars.

The pair fell into a sunken road, and surprised a platoon of camouflaged Gurkhas making their way up to the battle front. As one, the soldiers cocked their guns in a clatter of metal. As Adams had hoped and predicted, they stayed their trigger fingers a fraction from firing.

The young English lieutenant in charge of the group advanced slowly on them, his pistol trained alternately on Thacker's forehead and Adams' heart. He'd had a briefing, and frankly hadn't believed a word of it. Now, he wasn't so sure.

'Who goes there?' he asked, his voice betraying his nerves.

'Major Thacker, Chemical Weapons Unit, Porton Down.'

'Private Adams. Formerly of the Third Battalion, Durham Light Infantry.'

The officer brought the muzzle of his gun up to vertical. 'Sir? We were told to look out for you, but …'

'Where's Jack Henbury?'

'A mile over the rise. There were advance units, but they've now turned on us. We can't get close to him.'

'How close is he to Banbury?'

'In the outskirts already. The situation is very confused. There are civilians everywhere: only some of them are trying to kill us.'

'Get me forward,' ordered Thacker. 'Adams? Off. Your work is done.'

'I'm sticking around. I need to find Master Robert.' Adams swung down and stood defiantly in front of Thacker.

'Didn't you hear? They've been converted. Robert Henbury belongs to Jack now.'

'I won't believe it until I've seen it with my own eyes. Master Robert would never give in to that thing.'

It was useless arguing with him. It would get Adams killed, but it wasn't a concern of Thacker's anymore. The lieutenant consulted briefly with a map, and pointed his way down the road.

'This leads right over the bypass and the railway line. The creature's last position was just beyond there.'

'You've been warned not to get too close,' said Thacker.

'Yes, but how close is that? We've lost contact with units well outside what we thought was the danger zone.'

'Leave Jack to me. Just get me that far.'

The lieutenant nodded, and they started off. Thacker thought the pace impossibly slow, but the Gurkhas were doing almost double-time.

They started to pass bodies. Soldiers, civilians, caught in the moment where they stopped trying to kill and instead had been killed. People: men and women, fathers and mothers, brothers and sisters, all now cut and torn and beaten and shot. They'd woken up that morning to beautiful warm sunlight, and wondered what the day might bring.

It brought them Jack Henbury, and they wouldn't see the sun set.

'I thought the artillery would be here by now,' said Thacker.

'It is. But they can't fire on Banbury.'

'Why not?'

'Good God, Major, we're trying to reduce the collateral damage, not shell built-up areas.'

'That's a mistake.'

The lieutenant looked sideways at Thacker. 'How can you say that?'

'Because I've felt him in my head.'

'Oh.' The hedges either side of them suddenly stopped. The road continued out over a bridge which spanned first a four-lane carriageway, then a pair of electrified train tracks.

There was nothing moving on the Banbury ring road. It was blocked with burning and crashed vehicles, smoke and glass, and spilled loads from jack-knifed lorries and burst vans.

Beyond, where the road dipped down into the heart of a down-at-heel council estate, there were more fires, the sounds of breaking and exploding, of screaming and shouting, of shooting and bloody riot.

And briefly, in the gap between two houses, Jack Henbury's bizarre figure could be seen, the air, the very fabric of reality rippling around him. Then he was gone.

The lieutenant turned to Thacker. 'Do you honestly think you can kill him, dressed in that?'

'I think that if I can't, no-one can.'

'I only ask, because I'm going have to risk the life of every man here, and frankly, you look damn strange.'

'Forget what I look like. I carried Adams on my back all the way from Henbury Hall, and I'm not even out of breath.' Thacker felt better than that. He was itching to do battle, almost desperate to prove what he could now do. No more beating his head against trees for him. He would close with Jack, spit him with his spear and crush his spindly neck.

'Right.' He waved his point man on to the exposed bridge. He was halfway across, above the bank that separated the road and the railway. He stopped, and beckoned them on.

The rest of the platoon started over. The man on the bridge raised his rifle and shot three of them dead before the others could scramble back.

The lieutenant lay flat on the tarmac, his head just below line-of-sight. He shouted angrily at Thacker: 'Is this too close? How can this be too close?'

Thacker got to his feet, his soldier's instincts too great to overcome his new-found sense of invulnerability. 'It's certainly too close now. Jack's powers have got stronger. It's up to me, now.'

He started running, faster, faster. The figure on the bridge was firing at him. He could see the muzzle flash, and feel the impact of the bullets as they thundered against his out-thrust shield.

He hit the Ghurkha with the shield boss as he passed, barely breaking step. The man was flung back against the bridge's metal railings. He didn't stop to look, or even glance behind him. He knew he'd killed him with one blow.

He slowed as he got to the other end of the bridge. At

the T-junction, the road that went right petered out into a wasteland of old, abandoned cars and fly tipping. The one that went left was a scene straight from the deepest circle of Hell.

There were bodies, much like the ones he'd already seen. He was ready for that. The burning houses and cars, likewise. He'd practised civil riot control and military urban combat. He'd simulated throwing up a cordon around a contaminated site and shooting mothers and children who tried to breach the wire.

He'd caught a small taste of what to expect at Henbury Hall, when he'd first tried to shoot Jack. There on the streets of an English town, it hit home what life with their new god might be like.

There were hundreds of people facing the towering figure at the far end of the street. Some were lying down before him, calling for mercy that would never come. Some were standing, cutting themselves with knives and glass, calling out their pain and devotion, desperate to show their zeal. Some were turning on their fellow worshippers, singling out one person for their lack of faith, and beating them to death for their faults.

Others were committing the most degrading, bestial acts they could imagine, and offering up their deeds as a sacrifice.

Thacker's ancient suit of armour didn't amplify his courage, either. He swallowed hard on a dry mouth and felt suddenly very cold.

Jack seemed to look up, to notice him, through the beatific haze of adoration. He turned his strange body, and craned his neck to get a better look. Something of his puzzlement was communicated to his diabolic congregation. They started by looking over their shoulders at him, and ended by facing him.

Thacker could barely look at them, their bloodied and tear-streaked cheeks, their eyes without a spark of hope, their bodies given up to serve their capricious master.

From somewhere, he found his voice.

'Jack Henbury? I've come for you.'

A knot of pressure built up in his skull, but it faded. It was not like before, now he was protected. A thin, reedy sound drifted over the silent crowd. At first, he couldn't tell what it was. Then he started to hear words.

'What are you? Why do you not bow before Me?'

'Why? Because I'm going to kill you, you freak, that's why. I've already destroyed the machine. When I'm done with you, I'm going after the Ankhani, one by one.'

'You cannot defy Me. I am your god.'

'I've defied you once already, and I'll do it again.'

'Then,' said Jack, 'you are My enemy, and I must crush you like I have crushed all opposition to My rule.'

With that, the mob began to edge forward, their faces contorted with fear and superimposed rage. They picked up weapons: bricks, paving slabs, wooden posts and metal bars, broken bottles and building tools. A few had guns, and they aimed them at Thacker.

Perhaps he could have beaten them all, lunging through the middle of them, swinging his spear and his shield. He would be a great bronze giant ploughing through a sea of demented people, breaking their skulls, piercing their ribs, trampling them underfoot. They would try to cling on, bring him down and probe his armour for weak spots, looking for an unguarded place through which to slip a thin knife.

He didn't wait for them to reach him. He turned and ran. He knew he could outpace them, and by the time he stopped to take stock at the T-junction, the vanguard of his pursuers were already twenty yards behind.

He cut left onto the Banbury Road, but almost immediately went left again. He jumped a garden fence, and was suddenly alone. Climbing onto a coal bunker, he leapt into the next garden. Behind him, he could hear both horrified consternation and abject apology as the mob tried to explain to Jack that they had lost sight of the metal-encased man. By the sudden screams and wails, he was not placated.

Thacker kept working his way up the row of houses until he was sure he had Jack between him and the mass of crazed worshippers. He stepped between two of the houses and made his way to the street.

Jack had his back to him. He was selecting people at random and pitching them high in the air, watching them fall broken-backed to the concrete. The survivors covered their ears uselessly against the mental blast and wept, because it was not them that had been chosen.

Thacker hefted his spear and watched the flag flutter, checked the dented lion aspect of his shield, and started walking towards the god.

It was then that he noticed, sheltering by Jack's feet, two men. One was naked, bowed, filthy, balanced on only one leg, his hands tied tight behind his back and his neck in a noose. The other end of the rope was held by a man in a tattered and soiled suit, one shoe on, the other missing.

It was Dickson, and his prisoner was Robert Henbury.

The ministry man just happened to glance round as Thacker approached. Certainly, he couldn't have heard him through the noise. He almost turned back, his eyes not believing what they were seeing. He brought up his pistol, and instinctively Thacker threw his spear.

It was a throw worthy of a hero. The broad leaf blade slammed completely through Dickson, and out the other side, the red, white and blue cloth tied to it turned violent crimson. Dickson sank to his knees and pitched over onto his side. The gun clattered to the floor, and at that, both Henburys looked round.

Thacker didn't hesitate this time. He put his head down and charged.

# 11

He felt time expand. Thacker wasn't given to moments of pure, unadulterated terror, but he knew that this was what it was like. The only other time had been the two seconds he'd had to stop a balaclavered man from dropping a flask full of plague down a ventilation shaft and into the London Underground.

Two seconds, and he'd unholstered his Browning, emptied the full clip into the man's chest, and still managed to catch the stoppered bottle before it had fallen a foot.

Everyone except himself moved like they were imbedded in glass. Robert Henbury was still open-mouthed at the death of his immediate captor. Jack Henbury was projecting waves of hate at him, even as he struggled to bring his body around.

Thacker watched Jack's left foot rise uncertainly, and dived for his right. Mid-flight, he discarded his shield and stretched out both hands for the thin leg.

He connected. How could he fail to? The god span and fell, like a sawn-through tree.

Then time restarted. All the noise and confusion and enormity of what he had done rushed in on him. Unlike the moment in the dark tunnel under the capital, Jack was more than capable of striking back.

Strike he did. The road heaved up in a fountain of stone, blasting Thacker free of his grip. Landing on his back, Thacker kept rolling until he was upright. The houses either side of the street fell in on themselves and roared towards him in a tidal wave of debris.

He jumped back, onto the roof of a car caught up in the flood. It swung and bucked unpredictably, crushed below and sinking. The sea of rubble stopped heaving, and a street light launched into the air like a rocket and arced towards him.

He dodged the great length of steel as it whistled through the car roof and deep into the rock below. Jack got to his feet, slowly, ungainly.

A rumbling beneath him warned him a fraction of a second before another stone fountain ripped the road surface in two. He was showered with earth and cobbles, and was forced back. Jack advanced a step, and the tactic was repeated. No sooner had the last eruption ceased than a new one began, and Thacker was always on the back foot, holding his arms above him to protect himself from the hard rain.

Jack collapsed the last houses in the row, using the rubble to form a bank, then added to it until it became an unstable rampart. He set fires in the other houses, and they quickly began to burn with acrid, black smoke.

He'd trapped Thacker, who'd retreated just about as far as he could. He gathered his powers, and the road surface began to steam.

Thacker looked for a way out. He'd cause an avalanche if he tried to scale the wall of loose stone behind him. It would bury him, and by the time he could free himself, Jack would be able to do anything to him. He could run through the burning buildings to either side. And Jack would drop the first storey on him, and the result would be the same.

He'd made a mistake right back at the very start. He

should have thrown his spear at Jack, not Dickson. He'd not get a second chance.

Robert Henbury would, though. He'd cut through his bonds with the bloodied blade of the spear. No-one had the wit to stop him, they were so in awe of their god's manifestations.

As the tar melted, and Thacker felt his feet begin to burn, Robert Henbury used what little strength he had left to lift the spear up, and to drive it into the back of his cousin's knee.

Whether it was pain or the sheer surprise of being assaulted by the last person he considered to be a threat, Jack's concentration broke. He'd never controlled Robert. He wanted him to see everything, to suffer the unique fate of being a conscious witness to the world's end. Now, Robert twisted the spear haft and drove the point deeper.

Thacker, his boots sinking in molten tarmac, tore himself free and flung himself forward. The air shimmered, blinding him, moving Jack away.

Not trusting his false vision, Thacker went by faith alone. He grabbed something that gave, and twisted with all his might.

The god toppled again.

Thacker pulled the spear free and swarmed up Jack's body like a brass beetle. He stabbed at his shin, his injured knee, his thigh: quick blows meant to disorientate, not disable.

Jack was looking at him over his prostrate body. As Thacker raised the spear again to bring it down in the thin grey skin over the stomach, an incredible force deflected it aside.

He wrestled with the shaft, trying to bring it back into line. Every muscle was knotted like a cord, and the joints of the suit groaned. They were locked together. Jack even brought up his misshapen arms and started batting Thacker's back. Physical strength was not his forte, and Thacker hardly noticed.

The point of the spear bore down, slowly but inexorably. It punctured the altered flesh, and Jack writhed and howled in a distant, high whine.

Thacker was suddenly struck blind. The shock of it, the almost audible pop inside his skull, made his whole body spasm. The spear bit deep, then his hands flew to his eyes. He was thrown clear, landed hard on his back, and everything was still dark. He tried to listen above the hoarseness of his breath, the thundering of his pulse in his ears: Jack's wail kept on and on, slowly fading away. The sound of burning – bursting glass, cracking timbers, collapsing floors and ceilings – took over.

Someone was picking at his visor, probing for unseen catches.

'Who's that? Who's there?' He ought to get up, because the mob was still there, and still baying for his blood. But where would he go, and how would he get there? He couldn't see.

'Lie still, man,' said a familiar voice.

'Henbury? Robert Henbury?'

'There. That's done it. Yes, it's … Good God. Major Thacker.'

'Why can't I see?'

'You've blood everywhere. Don't tell me that you didn't get that head wound seen to.'

'There wasn't time. There was never time.'

'You ought to have made time. You almost had him.'

'Jack? Where is he?'

'Staggered off, holding his guts in. A moment.' Henbury's voice lessened, then came back. Something soft, but faintly gritty, was used to wipe the blood away.

Thacker's vision cleared to the point where he could blink and see a shape leaning over him.

'What are the others doing?'

'Currently, standing there watching us. Thacker, the things I've seen. I thought the trenches were bad, but if I wasn't mad before, I certainly am now. I never imagined such depravity.'

'Will they attack us?'

'I don't know. I could ask.'

'No, don't. Don't provoke them. If they're still under Jack's influence, they'll just be waiting for the order.'

Henbury continued wiping. 'I wish I had some water. Is this some sort of British secret weapon you're wearing?'

'I think it's Babylonian. I found it in the Ankhani's cathedral. I destroyed the machine, by the way.'

'I'm grateful.'

'I can almost see.' He could even make out the pattern on the blood-spattered curtain. 'Help me up.'

'I can't lift you.'

'Of course you can't.' Thacker sat up, and squinted into the blur that was all that was left of his eyesight. 'The spear. Where's the spear?'

It clanked along the ground, and was put into his hands. He climbed to his feet, and it seemed further than he remembered it. He was unsteady, wavering.

'Steady, Major.'

'What's happened to me? Why can't I see properly?'

'I think you've damaged your brain, broken the skull at the front. Pressure inside is pushing against your optic nerve. There were men like you in the field hospital, back in Belgium.'

'What happened to them?'

'Died of fever. We almost all did. Has eighty years brought anything to help?'

'If I got to a hospital, the doctors could certainly save me, and probably my sight.' Thacker blinked hard. 'We have Jack to deal with. If he can heal himself, all this was useless.'

Henbury used Thacker to climb up and lean against. 'My foot's cut to ribbons. I can't go any further.'

'You have to.'

'None of this was my fault.'

'I know. We're just the ones who have to clear it up.'

'I can't. I'm sorry.' Henbury sat down again. 'Straight on. Down the road. Jack's in the scrub at the far end. I'm sorry, Major, I'm sorry.'

Thacker found himself walking. Shadowy figures moved aside for him as he approached, and one man called out to him.

'What are we supposed to do now?'

'Do? I think you've probably done enough for one day. Go home.'

'We haven't got homes anymore.'

'That's a shame.'

'But what are we going to do? When will we get help?'

'I saw what you did. Never would be too soon.'

'I didn't have a choice.'

'You did it because deep down in your foetid little soul, that's how you always wanted to behave. Jack just let you be your true self. I don't care what happens to you. Not now.' He walked on, the crowd thinned, and was eventually behind him.

Before, he could sense where Jack was. Perhaps he could do it again. He closed his eyes, concentrated, and found him, weakly, an incoherent mass of pain and rage. With his sight failing him, he instead followed his preternatural instinct.

The track that led into the scrub was strewn with rubbish. It tripped and snagged at Thacker's feet. There were old plastic sacks, broken windows still in their frames, pallets and piles of building rubble. Cars, without seats, wheels, paint, hunkered down amongst the riotous weeds. Newspapers, discarded articles of clothing, polystyrene fast-food containers and used condoms littered the brambles and nettles. Trees had seeded freely for fifty years.

Somewhere in that dense, overgrown thicket was Jack Henbury, licking his wounds.

Thacker couldn't see. He saw only a mess of shifting green and brown and black, shadows and light, playing indistinctly in his mind. But when he ignored what he saw and believed what he felt, it was like an arrow, pointing him to his target. He pulled down his visor, and was swallowed up in a heady mix of certainty and confusion. He advanced through the tree line, and started to hunt.

There was no sure footing, no silent approach, but he knew each step he took brought him closer to Jack. In a clearing, in the very centre of the tangled wood, he found him.

He had surrounded himself with a vortex of hissing leaves and soil. It obscured his outline, and made it impossible for Thacker to see him at all. He edged through, feeling the clatter of stones and twigs against his armour, then quiet again.

Jack twisted and contorted at the focus of the tornado.

He held his stomach with one hand, and his forehead with the other. He groaned and trembled, sighed and gasped.

'Time to finish this, Jack,' said Thacker, 'Time to put you out of your misery.' He raised his spear and jabbed at empty air.

'No,' hissed Jack. 'I am your god. It will never be over.'

The roar of spinning air deepened in tone, and trees started to creak. Whole branches were torn off, white wood flashing inside the dark bark.

Thacker changed tactics. He swung the spear blade from side to side, shuffling forward, until he hit soft skin and hard bone.

The tornado exploded outwards, lacerating the scrubland with sharp missiles. None of them were directed at Thacker. He swung again, and Jack, who had been standing over him, crashed backwards through the canopy of leaves.

'Do not strike Me. I am immortal.'

'We'll see about that.' He blundered on, kicking out with his metal-shod feet, waiting for a cry of indignation, then stabbing down with his spear. He found Jack's body, and brought the point down. There was no titanic struggle. The edges of the blade cut through divine tissue and holy viscera, and into the neglected earth of England below.

'No. I cannot die. I can not die. They promised Me.'

'They lied,' said a different voice. 'They always did.'

'Who's there?'

'Adams. I'll finish this, Major.'

Thacker could dimly perceive someone standing by Jack's head, his arm outstretched and pointing down. There had to be a gun in his hand.

'He's still dangerous, Adams. Watch out.'

'Not anymore. Are you, Jack? I can feel you worming around in my head, trying to control me, but you haven't got the strength. Have you, Jack? Where's your power? Where are your followers? I'm not one, and certainly not the Major. All alone again, aren't you? When you came to Henbury Hall, you brought nothing but misery with you. You betrayed Master Robert. You seduced Miss Emily. You lied to all of us, but you never supposed for one moment that what you were doing was wrong.'

He cocked his weapon. 'This is where the reckoning is, Jack. The Ankhani used you. You could no more control them than a dog can its owners. Poor, weak, stupid Jack Henbury dies alone and hated, his head full of dreams of empires and riches.'

Thacker screamed out, 'For God's sake, finish him off!'

Adams pushed the barrel of the gun between Jack's terrified eyes and pulled the trigger. And again. And again.

Each time, the body jerked.

The sense of Jack's presence that Thacker held in his head dissipated like a summer cloud. There was nothing in its place.

'Is he dead?' he called.

'There's nothing left of the top of his skull, if that's what you're asking. If he comes back from that, then yes, I'll bow to him.'

'Don't joke, Adams.'

'Poor taste, I know. Are you all right, Major?'

Thacker had sunk to his knees, only keeping himself upright with the impaling spear.

'Major?'

There was a crashing in the undergrowth around him, and he found himself surrounded by short, sallow figures. Voices foreign to him chattered excitedly, and an English tongue cut through them all.

'Careful with him, boys, careful. He's a hero.'

He was lifted up and turned. Strong shoulders supported him, and carried him away. Thacker's head rolled side to side with the motion of his bearers. He watched the smudges of light and dark dancing above him blend together, into one final shade of grey.

Thacker hadn't realised he had armed guards stationed outside his hospital door until Robert Henbury mentioned it.

'Big buggers they are, too. Black balaclavas over their heads, that black armour your police chappies wear.'

'They're your police too,' murmured Thacker. He looked at all the little lights and lines that told him that he was still alive. He put his hands down by his side to adjust his position – bloody pressure sores – and felt the tug of the drip tubes in his arms. 'It's good to see you.'

'I'm rather surprised they let me in.'

'You're one of the few people I can talk to about any of this. Even my family are off-limits until I get debriefed.'

'That's a shame.' Henbury took off his new lightweight glasses and swung them between thumb and forefinger. 'Adams sends his regards.'

'I'm surprised he's still talking to me. I didn't give him a particularly easy time.'

'I think he's forgiven you. More than the government has.'

'Well, yes.' Thacker had talked to an army lawyer that morning. Despite her breezy assurances that everything was going to work out for the best, he wasn't so sure. He'd killed Dickson and destroyed the machine: some people in MI5 weren't taking that lying down. 'Look, do you mind if we don't talk about that? It's all *sub judice* now, and I expect you'll be a witness at the Court Martial.'

'My dear chap, I don't think they'll let me get within ten miles of it. Nor Adams.' Henbury lapsed into silence, uncomfortable around all the paraphernalia of intensive care. 'I'm going to see Emily.'

Thacker made the effort to sit up.

'Are you sure?'

Henbury put his glasses back on. Thacker thought he looked years younger: surprising what some food, rest, and not having the threat of Ankhani hanging over his head had done.

'No. No I'm not. But I look at it this way. If I don't go, and the old girl dies, then I've missed my chance. We lost eighty years, thanks to my cousin. I don't see why we shouldn't have the last laugh. I'm going down tomorrow. Adams is coming too. He said he fancied a day at the seaside.'

'So they're treating you right? Not blaming you for what I did?'

'Actually, I think they're a bit scared of me. I'm not ashamed to use it to my advantage.' Henbury looked with concern at the pallid, drawn figure in amongst all the tubes and wires. 'You'd better get your rest, old chap.'

'Better so they can hang me sooner.' Thacker eased himself down with a groan. He felt trampled. The neurosurgeon had shown him the drill he'd used on Thacker's skull, and it wasn't even his head that hurt.

Henbury picked up his crutches and levered himself upright. 'A strange do, what?' he said with bemusement, and headed for the door.

'Do you ever think about what happened in Banbury?' asked Thacker suddenly. 'Those people ... the things they did.'

Henbury stopped. Without turning, he said: 'I was in the trenches. I'd already had a thorough education in what men can do to each other, thank you very much.'

'Dear God, I'm sorry.' Thacker burned with embarrassment. 'Robert? Get your revenge. Live long.'

Henbury twisted round on his one leg and smiled. 'I have every intention of doing so, Major.'

# About The Author

Dr Simon Morden, B.Sc. (Hons, Sheffield) Ph.D (Newcastle) is a bona fide rocket scientist, having degrees in geology and planetary geophysics. Unfortunately, that sort of thing doesn't exactly prepare a person for the big wide world of work: he's been a school caretaker, admin assistant, PA to a financial advisor, and a part-time teaching assistant at a Gateshead primary school. He now combines a busy writing schedule with his duties as a house-husband, attempting to keep a crumbling pile of Edwardian masonry upright, wrangling his two children and providing warm places to sleep for the family cats.

His not-so-secret identity as journeyman writer started when he sold the short story 'Bell, Book and Candle' to an anthology, and a chaotic mix of science fiction, fantasy and horror followed. *Heart* came out to critical acclaim, and *Another War* was shortlisted for a World Fantasy Award, but with *The Lost Art*, things suddenly got serious. Contracts. Agents. Deadlines. Responsibility. Scary stuff. *The Lost Art* was subsequently a finalist for the Catalyst Award for best teen fiction.

As well as a writer, he's been the editor of the British Science Fiction Association's writers' magazine *Focus*, a judge for the Arthur C Clarke awards, and is a regular speaker at the Greenbelt Arts Festival on matters of faith and fiction. In 2009, he was in the winning team for the Rolls Royce Science Prize. In 2011, the first three *Petrovitch* books were collectively awarded the Philip K Dick Award.

You can keep up with his latest exploits by visiting the infamous Metrozone at www.simonmorden.com.

# Acknowledgements

Two people made this book possible.

Many moons ago, Andy Fairclough accepted the original *Another War* for his online anthology *Masters of Terror*. This short story, subsequently renamed *A Forgotten Corner of Hell* and reprinted in the collection *Brilliant Things*, seemed to call to me for a resolution. Henbury Hall wanted to come back, and with a bang of several cubic miles of displaced air, it suddenly did.

Feverish scribbling ensued, and all I had to do then was find someone to publish it. David Howe never did get away: despite my inability to write a cogent synopsis, I finally wore him down to the point where he agreed to read the entire manuscript.

The results are in your hands. Gentlemen, thank you.